CW01276812

The

Bittern's Call

Sue Lumb

Matador
9 Priory Business Park,
Wistow Road, Kibworth Beauchamp,
Leicestershire. LE8 0RX
Tel: 0116 279 2299
Email: books@troubador.co.uk
Web: www.troubador.co.uk/matador
Twitter: @matadorbooks

ISBN 978 1789018 844

British Library Cataloguing in Publication Data.
A catalogue record for this book is available from the British Library.

Printed and bound in Great Britain by 4edge Limited
Typeset in 11pt Filosofia OT by Troubador Publishing Ltd, Leicester, UK

Matador is an imprint of Troubador Publishing Ltd

The Bittern's Call

For David,
for his support and encouragement
along the journey

1

Night

THE ROOM WAS STIFLING. Maggie could feel perspiration trickling down her face, plastering her hair to her forehead. Her mouth was dry. She was desperate for a cold drink of water, but she dare not move. Keeping her head as still as possible she tried to look at the clock, but it was impossible to focus on the luminous figures that danced and blurred. Cautiously she inched a hand to her face, careful not to disturb the sheets. Perhaps the damage wasn't so bad, but the tender swelling she could feel around her cheek and the realisation that her left eye was almost closed told her it was.

There was movement in the bed next to her. She held her breath. *Please don't wake up.* But he was stirring. She felt the mattress dip as he turned over and then the sheets lift as he reached towards her. A strong arm wrapped around her waist, pulling her towards him. She tried to resist but he was too strong; it was useless. It was always useless. She wanted to shout *'NO'*, but no sound escaped her parched mouth.

In her dream, the pain and fear evaporated away. She clung to her favourite toy, holding it carefully in her small hand. She stroked the carved mane and face of the tiny wooden horse, feeling the defined edges of its ears then tracing her fingers down its legs to the roughly shaped hooves. She could feel the silkiness of the wood, worn smooth from her touch. It didn't matter that one leg was broken off. It had been made especially for her and it was the most precious thing she had. She held it to her face and felt the comfort it always brought creep over her.

Maggie woke with a start. It was daylight. Her body was stiff and aching and her face throbbed. She eased herself over and found the bed next to her was empty. Adam had left for work. She let out a shuddering sigh of relief.

Sitting at the dressing table mirror, she stared at the sad creature before her. The image reflected how she felt; exhausted and drained. Her fine, mousey hair, always dull in her eyes, looked even more limp and lifeless, framing a tired, pale face. The dark ring beneath her right eye was familiar, but the left eye was still partially closed, redness already turning to purple; black would follow soon.

Going to work wasn't an option; she couldn't bear the endless questioning. *Maggie, what on earth have you done this time? It's okay to talk to someone you know, Maggie – tell me what happened.* To Maggie, those concerned voices were always trying in vain to disguise an insatiable desire for gossip.

Maggie made the call to the bank. Non-descript music played as she waited to be put through to her boss. She tried to remember what excuse she'd used last time. The music stopped.

"Hello, Maggie — it's Janet."

"I can't come in today. Sorry." It took no effort for Maggie's voice to reflect how she felt. Her voice was usually soft and timid. This morning, in her head, it sounded pathetic.

"What's wrong?" Her supervisor made no attempt to hide her irritation, but at least she managed not to add *'this time'*.

"Stomach bug. It came out of nowhere. I've been throwing up all night. I feel terrible."

A void of silence followed lasting endless seconds.

"Ok, well, there's nothing you can do about it. Feel better soon. At least it's Friday, so hopefully we'll see you on Monday."

Maggie knew Janet wasn't convinced. It was hard to lie. But the truth was so much harder. To speak the words out loud would be to admit what her life had become.

"Thanks."

"Maggie, are you sure everything is all right? Are you certain I can't help you in any way?"

Janet had mastered her annoyance and now her voice communicated nothing but concern. In the face of such sincerity, Maggie felt her resolve weaken. Should she tell someone? In the fraction of a second that followed, the briefest of moments in time, Maggie's head was filled with conflicting thoughts. She could imagine the relief of releasing the secrets she had kept for so long. Of perhaps finding someone who might help her. Then the fear and shame enveloped her once more and flushed away the tiny seed of hope.

"No, I've got everything I need, thanks," Maggie said, ignoring the real meaning behind Janet's question.

"Okay – if you're sure." Janet rang off.

Maggie put the phone down and burst into tears. When the sobs finally subsided, she sat on a high stool at the breakfast bar, holding a mug of coffee in hands that refused to stop shaking. She gazed around the modern, high-tech kitchen, gleaming and shining in its sterile beauty. It looked like an advert on television, she thought. In fact the whole flat looked like that; contemporary and minimalistic, with polished floors and brightly coloured leather chairs and sofa. Huge windows, shaded with fancy blinds, looked out across the city. It was light and bright and perfect. And it had no soul.

Maggie looked around, dismally aware that apart from her personal things, not one item was hers. Everything belonged to him. She lived with Adam and she was allowed to share his possessions. And then the pain of the deeper reality stung her. It wasn't just material things that belonged to Adam. She belonged to Adam. Her life was limited by the boundaries that he set.

She reached across to the radio and switched it on in the hope that music would lift her spirits. Her favourite song from 1983 was halfway through and she was instantly transported back to that brief time of happiness and hope — just three years before. She turned the radio off as fresh tears spilled onto the smooth grey work surface. She was tired. Maggie was twenty-one and she felt old.

Sliding down from the ridiculously high stool, she snatched up her car keys and bag and took the lift down to the garage. There, sad and rusting, was the only thing that belonged to her. With no destination in mind, she started up her old Escort and drove away.

2

Langley

IT WAS RUSH HOUR and the city roads were jammed. Buses and cars jostled for position at every junction, exhaust fumes swirling like steam between the vehicles. Without knowing she had done it, Maggie wound up her window against the pervading toxic gas. She drove as though in a trance, reliving the terrors of the night before. Junctions, traffic lights and roundabouts all came and went without her having any memory of negotiating them. Eventually the city centre gave way to greener, leafier suburbs, where expensive houses lined either side of the road, becoming grander by the mile. Where open countryside finally beckoned, a scattering of exclusive mini mansions appeared, each perfectly placed in extensive gardens; ornate gates barring access to alien lives.

As she drove away from the city, the torment of the past years enveloped and overwhelmed her. This was not the life she had planned and, despite what her father said, it was not the life she deserved. An image of her mother's face came into her mind – the image. It was the only one she could remember clearly without looking at photographs. When she thought of that face, the soft brown curls and shining hazel eyes, she knew the life her mother had kept hidden from everyone behind that kind smile. Maggie had been too young to understand, but now she knew. *She would have helped me,* Maggie thought, as the tears flowed again, blinding her. She wiped them away, forgetting her battered face. Startled by the pain, she allowed the car to drift across the carriageway. The blazing headlights and fierce blaring horn of an on-coming vehicle jolted her to attention and she swerved back. Pulling into a lay-by she sobbed again, tears of desperation and of self-pity. She had nowhere to go and no-one to care if she lived or died. For a while she sat, numb with misery, as traffic thundered by; an endless stream of nameless people going about their daily business, oblivious to her pain. She glanced at her wing mirror, and through blurred eyes spotted a huge articulated lorry approaching from behind. Light reflected from its windscreen, shielding any view of the driver. To Maggie it was nothing more than a lifeless machine that could become her saviour. If she could just do it; all it would take would be a foot to the accelerator and a sharp turn of the wheel – and then it would all be over. No more fear; no more pain; no more life. She revved the engine and gripped the wheel tight, her knuckles turning white…but she couldn't do it. She was too scared; too scared to do anything. The truck hurtled past.

For several minutes Maggie sat, still clutching the wheel, unable to put the car in motion. She felt emotionless and empty and with that hollowness came eventual calm. When she finally felt composed enough to move on, she knew it should be to make the return journey. She could hear Adam's voice in her head commanding her to go home. But she resisted, and instead continued on, pulling off the main road and heading out into open country.

Maggie's love of the countryside was as strong as her dislike of towns. The city choked her; the noise, the crowds, the fumes, the unending drabness. And yet town life was all she had ever known. Now, as the lane climbed to the top of a gentle incline, rolling hills opened up on all sides, and she felt her spirits lift. The city was devoid of seasons, but here spring greeted her. Beech trees cloaked in fresh new leaves shone bright green in the sun and clumps of yellow primroses clung to sheltered banks by the roadside. Maggie tried to fix her mind on the sights around her, but as she drove, somewhere in the back of her mind, Adam's voice continued to nag at her. Still she moved onward, taking random turns and not caring where she was or where she might end up; all she felt was the compulsion to go forward.

It was only as she climbed higher, winding along wooded hillsides, and leaving villages of thatch and honey-coloured stone behind, that she realised she had reached the downs. She looked at her watch. Two hours had passed and almost seventy miles were behind her. The car came clear of the treeline, and grassy hills, mottled with chalky patches and cloud shadows, opened up on either side. Half a mile further, and a small parking area off the lane came into view. Maggie pulled in and turned the car around to face the way she had come.

The old Escort rested and as the engine idled, it spluttered and coughed and threatened to stall. Maggie looked at the temperature gauge; the car was over-heating. She thought of Adam's Audi – it never sounded like this. Her mind urged her to start the return journey, but her body froze, unwilling to comply. She looked wearily at the petrol gauge and assessed that she had just enough fuel to get home, that was if the engine kept going. "*Home,*" she whispered the word bitterly. There was no chance of getting back without letting the car cool. She switched off the ignition and opened the door, taking in deep breaths of fresh air. A cool breeze rolled over the high downs, and though the April sun was warm on her skin, she shivered. She stepped out and stretched her stiff body, becoming properly aware of her surroundings for the first time.

A rusted metal post, leaning precariously into the road, had a sign attached to it that read 'Footpath to Langley Manor'. It pointed to a chalky track leading up over the open downs. Maggie locked the car and set off along the path, convinced a short walk would do her good. For a few moments she felt exposed and alone. The small car park was empty and there was no one else in sight, but the uneasiness quickly lifted and she was aware that for the first time in a long time, here in this remote place, she felt safe.

The path continued over the brow of the hill, the grassy pastureland, mottled with orchids and cowslips, spreading out in all directions. A pair of skylarks gave brief escort, singing fluidly in flight as they rose from the edge of the path. She watched them until they were dots in the sky, shading her eyes from the sun, a glimmer of a smile touching her bruised lips.

At the top of the incline, the land fell away abruptly into the wooded valley below. From the right, a river ran along the valley floor; glimpses of flowing water shimmering through the trees. To the left, the wood thinned onto a vast area of flat grassland, the river twisting through it like a silver snake. On the far side of the valley, the forest covered the entire length of hillside opposite.

Maggie peered down the steep, stony track. At least she had put on jeans and trainers, she thought, and with no further hesitation set off down. Running and sliding on the stones, it took her less than fifteen minutes to reach the bottom of the hill. There the path guided her to the edge of the meandering river. Following the track by the water, she set off across the many acres of open grassland, surrounded by grazing sheep, and large long-horn cattle. She had never seen the breed before and for a moment, noting the unnerving curved and sharply pointed horns, wondered if she should be scared. But the three cows closest to her continued to graze without lifting their heads and showed no interest in her at all. She picked up her pace and hurried on past them.

A combination of exercise and warmth of the valley floor, now sheltered from the breeze of the higher ground, eased Maggie's tender body as she walked. She breathed in the scent of the countryside, the smell of grass and cattle mixing with the sweet aroma of hawthorn blossom. Her mind drifted and from nowhere she recalled a lost memory from her childhood. She had been six or seven and her school class had been asked to do drawings of their family. Maggie could remember her picture, coloured in vivid wax crayons. She was standing with her mother and father in front of their house; except it wasn't the semi-detached on the council estate where they lived. Instead they were standing before a small thatched cottage, with sloping walls and tiny windows. She had never seen a thatched house before but she could imagine what it should look like. It was surrounded by green hills and woods, with cows and pigs and chickens fenced in close by. It wasn't reality she had drawn – only the life that even then, as a small child, she dreamed of.

Maggie smiled sadly at the memory. If only she had never met Adam; if only she'd held back from rushing into the first real relationship she'd had; if only she had heeded the warning signs. 'I promise you, Maggie,' he'd said, 'a year from now we'll be married, out of this flat and out of the city.' She had been naïve to believe him. She had been in love. Back then she thought the kind of life she had dreamed of was within reach; raising a family away from the suffocating city with a man she loved and who loved her.

She knew now that Adam had never intended leaving; that he'd never intended marrying her. And Maggie had lost much more than three years of her life. She remembered being told once that a frog will boil to death and not jump out to save itself if the water is heated slowly. It occurred to her that she was the frog. As Adam had slowly revealed his true face, she had accepted him and what life gradually became with him. But then something had changed. Maggie put a hand to her stomach and felt the hollow, empty surge of longing. He had turned up the heat to more than she could bear.

The frantic cackle of startled coots flapping away from the riverbank drove the thoughts from her mind. The river had taken a sharp turn to the right, the view obscured by alders and willows along its banks. Maggie knew she was heading to somewhere called Langley Manor, but it still came as a surprise when, rounding the bend, the ancient house stood before her on the other side of the water.

3

The Oak Tree

A HOT FLUSH OF embarrassment flooded over Maggie. She was certain she had walked too close to the property and must be trespassing on private land. Even standing alone in the open, she was overcome by self-consciousness. Her face burned as she glanced about; she was convinced someone would appear at any moment and order her to leave. Then she was enveloped by a powerful and comforting sensation – that even though she didn't know this place, she was somehow welcome here.

She stared across at the medieval house, which was partially obscured by three exotic looking cedar trees. It was clearly an ancient building, its half-timbered walls bulging and sloping; distorted with age. The upper floors each projected out over the level below and its roof of red tiles shone bright in the sun. Standing face on, the building was made up of a central rectangular block, which sat back, and a north and south wing projecting forward at either end.

She guessed there were at least four floors, though the lower levels were hidden by a high garden wall. The wing to the south, on the right, had fallen into complete ruin – roofless and sad. As Maggie stared, fascinated, it seemed to her that the old house gazed back, watching her with equal curiosity through its many leaded windows.

As captivated as she was by the building, Maggie found her eyes drawn to the wooded hillside beyond, which rose steeply behind the manor. Despite her conviction that she shouldn't be there at all, Maggie felt an irresistible urge to venture closer. It was as though an invisible thread was pulling her forwards.

In the distance to her left, she could make out a single-arch stone bridge where a private road crossed the river and, for the first time, she saw people. A small group were walking along the road towards the crossing, and another couple were heading in the direction of the manor. It was a relief to see she might not be trespassing after all.

From the bridge, Maggie could now see that she was standing within a vast area of parkland that must belong to the house. The river ran on to her left, splitting into two channels either side a long, narrow island and here the banks gave way to a wide expanse of boggy marshland. For perhaps a mile or more, the pastureland on either side ran on a slight slope down to the river, but instead of meeting the defined edges of a riverbank, the green grass was engulfed by dense, impenetrable reed beds.

Maggie followed the road towards the manor, looking away as a middle-aged couple passed by with a breezy 'good morning'. She turned her bruised face from them, aware that she must have appeared rude. She could hear the couple whispering and, although she did not see, she was certain that they looked back and watched her.

As she approached the walled grounds, there were signs on wooden posts here and there, suggesting that the manor was open to the public some of the time – though with so few people about, clearly not on this day. One such sign read 'Langley Edge Woods' and pointed to the tree-covered ridge behind the manor. The hillside ran north to south for several miles and formed a natural and dramatic backdrop to the house nestled at its base.

The worry that she could not linger too much longer nagged at Maggie. The thought of Adam getting home before her, and having to explain her absence, filled her with dread and the ever-present knot tightened in her stomach – and yet she was still overwhelmed by the magnetic pull of the place and without further hesitation she pressed on.

The winding climb took a little over thirty minutes, and Maggie staggered out onto a flat grassy area at the top, gasping for breath and a little ashamed at her lack of fitness. A bench made from a split tree trunk provided both a resting place and somewhere to sit and admire the view of the valley below. Three men in their sixties, wearing hiking boots and with backpacks laid on the ground were spread out along the seat. They were taking a lunch break and nodding friendly greetings, shuffled along to make room for her.

"Come and have a sit down, love," one of them said with a friendly smile. "It's a bloody steep climb, isn't it?"

"I'm fine thanks," Maggie murmured, wiping the sweat from her face as she hurried past. "I'll carry on."

One of the men, who appeared to be the oldest of the three, had a kind, open face, and smiled at her.

"Well, why don't you have a drink and take a bite to eat with you?" he said, reaching into his pack. "Looks like you didn't bring anything with you." He poured some water into a plastic cup and passed it to her, along with an oat biscuit in a wrapper.

Maggie hesitated. She was thirsty and had been ignoring hunger pangs for some time. She took the offerings from him, feeling like a timid dog tempted by a treat.

The man was wearing a cap, the peak pulled down. He pushed it back from his eyes as though to get a clearer view and peered at her with curiosity.

"Are you all right – you're not in any trouble, are you?"

Maggie knew that he'd noted her face, which must by now look worse than it had in the morning. She forced a thin smile, though her voice trembled as she spoke.

"Just a bit of an accident, that's all. I wanted to get out for some fresh air."

The man didn't look convinced.

"What kind of accident would that be?" His question was motivated by concern, Maggie knew that. Still it irritated her.

"A bit of a car bump yesterday – that's all," Maggie said, the lie coming easily.

"Well, as long as you're sure you're all right."

"I am, thanks very much," she said. Then gulping down the water as quickly as she could, she passed the cup back and hurried away.

Several footpaths radiated away from the summit of the hill, and for no reason other than it was the quickest escape from view of the three walkers, she took the closest. She had followed the path for no more than twenty yards, when she noticed a narrow, unmarked trail almost hidden by the hanging branches of a twisted yew tree. Clearly it wasn't the main path and she passed it by, but then hesitated, drawn back. She ducked under the low branches, brushing fine spider webs from her face, and discovered that the track ran south, parallel to the hillside about twenty or thirty feet from a rocky edge. Glimpses of the parkland and marshes below could be seen through the budding trees and bushes.

As she walked, Maggie was struck by the contrast of where she found herself now, compared to the previous night. It was as though she had been lifted out of a terrifying nightmare, and placed gently into some kind of paradise. The trail weaved between oaks, beeches, birches, and yews. Wild spring flowers were already blooming on the light-filled forest floor, and everywhere was alive with birdsong; blackbirds, wrens, warblers, and now and again the distinctive laughing call of a green woodpecker.

Around a bend in the path, a huge and ancient oak tree came into view. She felt as if she had discovered a hidden and secret Eden. All her life she had felt adrift in an alien world, waiting to arrive at an unknown destination where she would feel she belonged. Somewhere like here. The thought brought a smile to her lips and warmth running through her insides. The sudden, stifling silence that followed was abrupt and startling. It was as though the change had been summoned by her feelings. Where moments before, the air had felt fresh and clear, now it became heavy and still. The birdsong stopped and the wood became utterly quiet.

Maggie stopped dead, every tiny hair on her arms stood on end as she stared up at the oak. It was like a giant sentry, stooped with age, but resolutely guarding the way; and it was massive. Limbs the size of other tree trunks branched from the main body; one curving almost to the ground before reaching skywards again. The vast trunk had hollowed out over the ages, and now a gaping hole on one side revealed a large boulder over which the tree had grown. The oak wasn't tall, it was just massive. The highest branches were dead and bare, standing like fleshless bones against the blue sky. Lichens and moss clung to the bark, and the budding twigs, now touched by the faintest of breezes, seemed to speak in ancient whispers.

Maggie walked to the trunk and reached out to touch it. As her fingers touched the rough bark, from the valley below came a strange and haunting sound, unlike anything she'd heard before. The sound reverberated, so deep as to be at the edge of hearing and yet penetrating – like the noise one might make by blowing over the top of a bottle. She listened, transfixed, and realised it was rising up from the marshes. The noise was followed by another and then another from different parts of the huge reed bed.

With the peculiar sounds and the even stranger atmosphere that had fallen upon the place, Maggie felt the first twinges of fear, and it was with relief that she heard people approaching. The voices were distant at first, and then, over the course of a few seconds, became clearer; coming closer. It was the sound of children playing. They were laughing and shouting and calling to each other excitedly. Maggie waited, still standing against the oak, as the squeals and chattering came closer. She expected to see the children through the trees and bushes ahead at any moment, but no one appeared. After a few seconds, the shrieks and calls faded as though they had turned away, and then, quite suddenly, stopped altogether. Barely a second passed before the silence was filled by the soft whispering of a man and woman speaking quietly together. The voices were very close, but Maggie could neither make out what they were saying nor see who they were coming from. All she could hear were hushed, tender murmurings, like lovers sharing a secret.

Maggie's stomach flipped as unease edged towards panic. She knew there were people around; she had seen the three men not too far away, and surely there would be others too, but she simply could not see from where these voices came.

The whispers faded away and silence returned for a moment only to be followed by the unmistakable sound of a woman crying. Gentle, muffled sobs giving way to desperate, uncontrolled weeping. It came from somewhere so close to Maggie, she could have reached out and touched the person if she could only see them. Her breathing became fast and shallow and she wanted to run, but her legs rebelled, fixing her to the spot. The sounds were right there, with her, and yet she was alone. A frightening weakness came over her and she leaned against the oak to steady herself, as a cascade of extraordinary emotions enveloped her. She was overwhelmed by feelings of happiness, joy, and love; all quickly surpassed by unbearable sadness and loss.

So shocking was the experience that for a moment she thought she would be physically sick, and then tears came from nowhere, coursing down her face, which she pressed hard against the bark of the tree. Painful sobs retched from some unfathomable place within her, and then, as quickly as they had surfaced the feelings subsided, giving way to a deep sense of peace and calm.

It was tranquillity unlike anything she had experienced before and seemed to spread into the air around her. For a time she could not measure, it was as though she had been transported to another world; a serene and soothing place.

Sunlight filtered down through the branches of the oak; the shadows dancing on her bare arms. A woodpecker drummed in the branches above, breaking the silence, and birdsong filled the wood once more. The spell was broken.

4

The Vacancy

MAGGIE'S LEGS FELT LIKE lead and she trembled as if she was cold. She looked around, a logical part of her still searching for the people she'd heard, though deep down she knew there was no one there. She stepped away from the tree and out of the peculiar, dream-like state. Taking a few paces to the edge of the steep hillside, she peered down. On the sloping ground the woodland was sparser, broken by rocky outcrops and loose boulders around which rowan trees and stunted birches clung. Here and there open spaces were filled with bluebells and tight bracken fronds.

At her feet, a flat rock jutted out almost into mid-air, and she sat down, dazed, but now completely unafraid. She was dimly aware that she must be having some sort of breakdown. She knew it in the same way that sometimes one might dream knowing that one is in a dream. She accepted it. After all she had been through, it was to be expected. She didn't care. She had no strength left to care about anything. Ignoring her mental state, she concentrated instead on the breathtaking view. She could make out what she guessed were the boundaries of the parkland, and beyond that the roofs of a village, nestling on the opposite side of the valley. Away to the left she could see the chalky track she had taken, like a thread of white cotton, weaving its way from the downs. Directly below, the cattle and sheep looked like toys in the vastness of the pastureland. To the right, perhaps a mile north of the manor, and sitting a little above the marshes, stood a lonely cottage surrounded by shrubs and trees, its stone walls golden in the sunlight. Maggie's breath caught and she felt a surge of longing. It looked so tranquil, so perfect, and she yearned to go to it. She dragged her eyes away from the cottage. From her elevated position, she could see that the parkland was not as flat as it had appeared from the valley floor. The sun cast shadows on the ridge and furrow workings of ancient field systems and the faint oblong traces of the remains of tiny buildings lost beneath the earth; clues to lives lived long ago – now lost and forgotten. The calls of cattle and sheep drifted up from the valley, but the reed beds were silent. The strange sound from the marshes had fallen quiet along with the other voices.

After a few minutes rest, Maggie got to her feet and prepared to start the journey back. It was hard to leave. The extraordinary events had left her feeling oddly rested and refreshed – somehow restored. Whatever it was that had happened, the place had had a profound effect upon her and as she walked away, leaving the stooped oak tree behind, she hoped more than anything that she might get the chance to return.

Maggie pulled into the car park beneath the apartments, thankful that the Escort had got her home, and even more relieved to see there was no blue Audi in the space next to hers. As she took the lift to the twelfth floor, Maggie was astonished at how different she felt. Only hours before, she had contemplated taking her own life. Now she felt *alive*. More than that − that this existence might have some purpose to it after all. She was infused with a sense of purpose and determination and, above all, the clear knowledge that her life had to change. She had no idea what those changes might be beyond an understanding of what must come first. She must leave Adam. Only after that could she create a better, more fulfilling existence for herself. The realisation brought with it a burning anticipation.

Adam was late, but that gave Maggie a chance to put her dusty clothes into the washer and clean her trainers; she must leave no clue that she had been out of the city. She put the stew she'd made the day before into the oven and then went to the bathroom to check her face. She was shocked. Her left eye was still half closed by the swelling and it was turning black. The bruising had darkened around her cheek and the side of her nose. Her lower lip was also swollen and the inside raw where her teeth had cut into it. Two days to improve, she thought, before she had to face work.

She heard the key in the door and her stomach lurched. She moved to the window and looked out. The flat faced south and she stared across the endless sea of rooftops, tower blocks, and spires, as she listened to Adam throw his keys onto the worktop and walk towards the bedroom.

Somewhere out there is Langley, she thought, and closed her eyes, imagining the sweet smell of the woods.

"Had a good day?" His voice was breezy. This was what he was usually like the day after.

"I didn't go to work." She wanted her voice to sound hard, accusing, but it didn't. It just sounded like Maggie.

"Oh, why not?"

Maggie closed her eyes again. *Why do you think?*

"I didn't feel well."

"What's wrong with you?"

She took a deep breath and turned round. There he was, tall and good-looking, taking off his suit trousers and pulling designer jeans onto long, lean legs.

"I didn't want anyone to see me like this."

Adam gave her a cursory glance and then looked into the mirror himself, combing his black hair back with long brown fingers. She watched him. How was it that she had once found those same hands so attractive?

"No need to be a drama queen. It doesn't look that bad to me." He turned around, a wide smile on his face. "Anyway, I've got some good news."

Maggie knew how to play the game; she had to push the bitterness and the fear from her mind and make an effort.

"Oh, what's that?" she said, sounding intrigued.

"The firm is merging with some tinpot company in London." She could tell he was buzzing with excitement. "There are going to be some promotions and..." he paused for effect, "... no guesses for who is in line for a top job at a second branch here."

"Oh, Adam, that's wonderful news." Maggie wondered where she found the energy.

"Yep, if I get it, I will be the youngest branch manager in the company."

"I'll open a bottle of wine to have with dinner," Maggie said, squeezing past him and heading towards the kitchen.

"Don't bother," Adam called after her. "I'm off out with the lads for a pre-celebration, celebration, if you know what I mean. Don't wait up."

Maggie watched him leave without a backwards glance.

She ate a little of the stew and threw the rest away, then she lay on the sofa. She was exhausted, but at least she would be able to rest easy for a few days. Adam would stay away from her for a while; it was something he always did following one of his violent episodes. It was as though he assumed that if he left her alone, she would somehow forget what had happened.

Over the weekend, Maggie's nights were filled with the sights and sounds of Langley. Her dreams were a slide show of images; the parkland and marshes with its haunting sound, the giant oak and mysterious voices, the lonely cottage by the reeds, her own small hands holding a toy horse. All the images merged and became part of a child's wax crayon drawing.

During the days, her mind was set to working out how to escape her life with Adam. It puzzled her why the idea of simply packing a bag and walking away had always seemed so impossible. She realised that she had been frightened of life without him – of being alone. More than that, she believed it was her fault that she endlessly disappointed him and she had tried so hard to be a better partner for him. His possessiveness had shown itself gradually during their first year together and had soon become the norm. But she remembered with stark clarity the first time he hit her. He had been sorry – just a flash of temper, that was all. And that's what he'd been like afterwards, every time. And all Maggie did was to try harder to please him. Any fight or strength had long since deserted her along with the last shreds of self-belief. That was until now. Now he had gone too far.

Maggie sat by the phone, staring at it as though waiting for it to ring. It was Sunday afternoon and Adam was out with friends. This was her chance to make the call, but she had picked up and replaced the receiver three times. Now she picked it up again and quickly dialled the number. As it rang, she felt her nerve evaporating and was about to put the phone down when a voice answered.

"Hello, Dad, it's me, Maggie." It was odd that she felt the need to give him her name as though she doubted he would recognise her voice.

"Not heard from you for a good while." There was the familiar brusqueness in his voice.

"No. Well, you know how it is. Time flies by." Even as she said the words, Maggie thought, *no – time doesn't fly; it drags by painfully, minute by minute.*

"Well – what can I do for you?" She could tell he wanted to say, 'what do you want?', but stopped himself.

Maggie struggled to say the words. "I just wondered if… I thought… or hoped you wouldn't mind if I came to stay for a while." Silence followed. She watched the second hand tick round on the wall clock. "Dad?"

"So, thrown you out has he?" His words were flat and devoid of emotion.

"No." Maggie took a deep breath, trying to control her voice. "But I need to leave him. I really need to get away." She wanted to scream down the phone at her father, *please, Dad, please just help me.* But she said nothing and waited.

"I told you not to go, but off you went and shacked up with him anyway, and without even the decency to get married – then hardly a word from you in three years." Anger rattled in his throat. "I haven't even seen where you live. And now because it doesn't suit you any more, you want to come back."

"I made a mistake, Dad. That's all I did – I just made a mistake." Her voice started to crack and she fought to control it. "And I've paid for it. I just want to make a new start."

"Well, you go ahead and make that new start – but don't think you can make it here." His voice hardened further and Maggie could picture the face she'd known all her childhood, thin lips pressed tight together, cold grey eyes focused on punishing the daughter who never failed to disappoint him. "Your mother would have been ashamed of what you've become – I'm glad she didn't live to see it."

No she wouldn't, she would have loved me. Maggie couldn't speak. There were no more words to be said. She put the phone down without saying goodbye.

Maggie tidied her desk top and headed to the upper floor of the three-storey building for her coffee break. She had withstood two days of questioning about her battered face and had stuck grimly to her story; she had passed out from the effects of the stomach bug, hitting her face against the bathroom sink in the process. She doubted anyone believed her, but it didn't matter. All that mattered to Maggie was that she didn't tell anyone what had really happened. The only saving grace was that she had been moved from the bank counter and spared having to face customers. As Janet, her supervisor, had put it, 'you can work in the back office, at least until you look a little more presentable.'

The large staffroom had a scattering of coffee tables and soft chairs, with coffee-making facilities to one side. As usual, Maggie sat alone at a corner table, buried in a novel. Other employees, many of whom she'd known for years by face if not by name, chatted away to each other, immersed in conversations that were always about the same things; films, television, sport, fashion, romances, and general gossip. Attempts to include Maggie were usually fruitless and most people had long since given up and ignored her. Today, the conversation revolved around some catastrophic event that had just happened at a nuclear power plant at a place called Chernobyl. The discussion in the room swung from 'it's nothing and will be forgotten in a day or two' to 'the entire world is doomed'. Maggie tried to shut it out.

Fifteen minutes later she started back down to the main floor before realising she had left her book behind. The staffroom door was ajar and she was about to enter when she heard someone mention the name – Adam.

"God knows why he's with her; he's a really good-looking bloke," a woman said. Maggie recognised the voice as someone who worked in the mortgage department.

"Well, you know what they say about the quiet ones," another woman quipped. "Hidden depths – if you know what I mean." Sniggers followed.

"Not enough depth from what I've heard." A man spoke this time.

"Come on – what've you heard, then?" the mortgage woman asked, her voice hushed with intrigue.

On the other side of the door, Maggie remained rooted to the spot.

"Well, not sure for certain, but he works for an insurance company. And I know someone who knows a guy who's just started work there." His voice became quieter but was still audible. "Apparently this Adam bloke has got a bit of a reputation – been having it away with at least two colleagues for most of the time he's been with… What's her name?"

"Maggie," mortgage lady offered helpfully.

"Don't be so horrible," a younger voice interjected. "I think he bashes her about."

"That wouldn't surprise me – she'd irritate the life out of me," the man said. More giggles.

Maggie stood frozen, her hand resting on the door handle. Someone else hurried past, pushing the door open to reveal her standing there. The room fell silent. She scuttled through without looking at anyone, picked up her book and left.

The next two hours were a blur. Maggie sat rigid at her desk, making mistake after mistake on her paperwork. She was convinced that every quietly spoken word was about her and that people who had no need to be in the office were there simply to peer at her. Lunch couldn't come quickly enough, and spot on one o'clock she rushed out of the building and headed to a nearby coffee shop where she could be free of prying eyes.

She sat with her drink, fighting back tears. She knew she wasn't as upset by Adam's actions as she was by the fact that everyone else appeared to know about it. After all, why should Adam's unfaithfulness come as a surprise to her? The woman at the bank was right. What did he see in her; what had he ever seen in her? It had always been a mystery to Maggie that an ambitious, handsome man had found her even remotely attractive. She didn't know and it didn't matter anyway. If what they said was true, then he had kept her at home as a useful outlet for certain needs whilst no doubt conducting himself as a true gentleman at work. What a fool she had been; a naïve, stupid fool.

A young woman came in pushing a pram and holding onto the reins of a toddler. She struggled to the table next to Maggie, trying to encourage the little boy to sit quietly whilst she positioned the pram.

Maggie got up to help. "Here, let me take him for a moment," she said, taking the little boy's hand. He looked up at her, grinning happily.

"Oh thank you so much," the woman said. "I didn't believe people when they said I'd had the second one too soon." She lifted the baby onto her knee where it started to grizzle and threaten to cry while she searched around with one hand inside the pram. Triumphantly she raised the lost dummy and popped it into the baby's mouth in the nick of time. "But now, I think they were right," she said laughing.

Maggie smiled and handed the toddler back, feeling the little hand slip from hers. She felt the pain tear at her insides and she sat with her back to them so she didn't have to watch them. Blindly she turned the pages of a magazine, cast aside on the coffee table, as thoughts of what Adam had done flashed through her mind and the sounds of the chattering child filled her ears

She turned the next page and stopped, staring in disbelief, her hand hovering in mid-air. Before her was a double-page photograph of Langley Manor. Not the Langley she had seen, but a photograph taken in winter, the landscape covered in thick snow; the forested hillside in the background, white with frost. For several moments, Maggie gazed at the image, tracing her finger across the picture as though touching it might magically transport her there.

She turned to the front of the magazine; it was a Sunday paper supplement on country houses of England and Langley was included along with several others. Over the page from the photograph, the article that went with it was fascinating. It told a little of the 600-year history of the manor and the Handley family who owned it, and then went into some detail about how running and maintaining the estate had changed over the centuries. Finally the piece described the latest developments and expansions to the Langley business, including the creation of a new garden centre and restaurant. Richard Handley said, '*We are delighted to have finally completed the new developments at Langley. They have taken longer than anticipated, and created a few planning and architectural headaches along the way, but I hope our visitors will enjoy the new facilities and find them in keeping with this beautiful old house. Buildings like this can only survive if they change with the times. Income from these new ventures will go towards our long-term plan to restore the south wing, which was gutted by fire over a century ago. We are also delighted that this expansion has created the opportunity for several new jobs on the Langley estate.*'

Below the article a list of job vacancies was shown. The advertisement was tiny, the smallest on the page. It was modestly headed 'Administration Assistant'. Maggie scrambled to turn the magazine to the front page, searching for the date; 20th April 1986 – last week. Her heart raced with excitement. Could she do it? The post itself read simply enough and would be within her capabilities. And it was Langley; the place that had captivated her so inexplicably just a few days before.

She was struck by the astonishing coincidence. It seemed incredible that she should go into that particular coffee shop where someone had left that magazine – and on this day of all days. She knew it was ludicrous, but to her it seemed that fate was playing a hand. Langley was searching for someone and Maggie needed somewhere to escape to. She read and reread the advertisement, particularly the last line, *Estate cottage available after six months.* She was being presented with the most unexpected and incredible opportunity for the new start she so desperately needed and she knew she must take it.

5

Chance of Escape

Maggie posted her letter of application for the vacancy at Langley the next day. At the same time she handed in her notice at the bank. Her actions were completely out of character. It was as though she had been possessed by an imposter; one prepared to give up a respectable job for an opportunity that was far from certain. She knew that most people would think her foolhardy, but no one understood her real circumstances. They guessed, but they didn't really know. And for once in her life, her mind was made up.

That evening she felt giddy with excitement and nerves as she made plans in her head. She had enough savings to tide her over for a few weeks. She would take a room at a bed and breakfast or find a bedsit — after all, she had no furniture, just her clothes and her car. She would agree a start date, organise some accommodation and leave. She wouldn't tell Adam where she was going — she would just be gone.

She hummed to herself as she prepared dinner. She needed to make it a special one. This was the day Adam would hear news of his promotion.

In the three years Maggie had known him, Adam had progressed swiftly at the insurance company. Starting as a clerk, he had acquired a taste for management and was already a junior manager when Maggie met him. She remembered seeing him for the first time. She had gone to a disco with some college friends – that was a time when she had friends. It seemed so long ago now. Since then, he had been promoted twice and was on course towards his goal of becoming a branch manager. Money and possessions were everything to Adam and he never doubted his ability to succeed. He was perfectly suited to the ambitious capitalism of 1980s Britain. He was only twenty-seven, six years older than Maggie, but the merger of his business with another company had brought with it the opportunity for further progression sooner than expected. Today was his interview and he had left for work with the cheery confidence that the outcome would be a foregone conclusion.

For Maggie the promotion was an unexpected bonus, something that was guaranteed to keep Adam in good spirits for weeks – *at least for long enough,* she thought. She had to stop herself from giggling out loud as she put the final touches to the meal, wondering how few more she would need to prepare for him.

Adam burst in, slamming the door behind him and throwing his case onto the worktop. Maggie felt every muscle in her body contract. Something was wrong.

"Those bastards don't know who they're dealing with." He yanked his tie from his neck and tossed it onto the floor.

Oh God, he didn't get it. It had never occurred to Maggie that such an outcome was even a possibility. She kept her back to him, laying the table, as she struggled for the right words. This was a crucial moment – she had to get it right.

"I'm sorry, love," she said, as gently as possible, bracing herself and turning to face him. "What happened? Don't tell me you didn't get the promotion."

He was across the kitchen in a flash, a flat hand striking her across the cheek, sending her sideways into the table. Crockery and cutlery crashed to the floor.

"Do I look like I got it, you stupid bitch?" He swept his hair back with one hand, running the other across his mouth. His grey eyes were clouded and Maggie could smell alcohol. He had already drowned his sorrows; now he was just angry. "It was mine, no doubt about it. Then they give it to some London idiot just to keep the bastards down south happy."

Maggie manoeuvred herself around to other side of the table, her face throbbing, a single tear trickling from the corner of her left eye. She was frightened to speak. It would be wrong to say nothing, but so would anything she said. Her mouth had gone dry and the blood pumped in her ears.

"There'll be other chances soon," she whispered, trying to subdue the panic rising from the pit of her stomach. "They know how good you are."

"They fucking will do. I'm a laughing stock. The shit I've had to take off the lads." He looked at Maggie, focusing on her for the first time. "You know how good I am, don't you?" He leaned on the table towards her.

"Adam, no... please... not while you're so angry."

He leapt forward, grabbing her arm and pulling her across the table towards him, the remaining crockery toppling to the floor. He pressed down on her small frame, forcing the breath out of her. For a fleeting moment she wondered if his lover would find him so attractive now. Then another dread filled her mind. What if she got the interview at Langley; how could she show up with a battered face? She forced herself to relax, fighting to give him no reason to beat her. It would soon be over. She closed her eyes and allowed the tranquil memories of the wood to fill her mind while he raped her.

───

Maggie waited to hear from Langley in an ever rising state of tension. Each evening she waited for Adam to return home, a sickening knot gripping at her stomach. For the entire week he remained in the foulest of moods in the mornings, but mercifully he left Maggie alone. Each evening he returned home late, but more relaxed and good-humoured than she could have hoped for. She suspected that he was finding solace with someone else. That unknown woman would never guess how grateful Maggie was to her.

Maggie had given the bank address for correspondence, and for a week she eagerly checked the post each morning – to find nothing. Doubt engulfed her. Unemployment levels were high and Maggie knew the job she had applied for would be attractive. What if she didn't even get an interview?

She was reassured by the thought that she would leave Adam anyway – go anywhere, just to be free of him. Still she waited and hoped, and that hope made her stronger. As each day dawned, the simple expectancy that she might hear from Langley lifted her spirits and numbed the physical pain that remained from Adam's last attack.

It took ten long days before she finally received what she was praying for – a letter inviting her to an interview the following week. She booked the day off from the bank and buried the letter deep in the bottom of her bag.

Time crawled by. Adam appeared to have bounced back from the shock of not getting the promotion. His state of mind was further improved having received news that the man promoted over him was, in Adam's words, 'a useless fuck'. He was convinced that it wouldn't be long before senior management realised their mistake and placed him in his rightful position.

Instead of Adam's happier mood putting Maggie at ease, her tension rose still further. She knew from bitter experience that his violent outbursts could emerge from a clear blue sky and she was on constant guard. On the evening before her interview, Adam came home and she immediately sensed a change. He was subdued and moody. Maggie felt sick. She could not – she would not, allow him to beat her, allow him to ruin her chances, and for the first time in a long time, she made the first move.

After their evening meal, Adam stretched out on the sofa to watch *Cheers*. It was the only television programme he watched that Maggie enjoyed, and this evening, instead of sitting stiffly next to him, she curled herself up against him. When the programme had finished, she leaned over and kissed him gently. She stroked his cheek and ran her fingers down his throat and chest in soft caresses. At last he responded and she eased herself onto him, relaxing her body and allowing him in gently. When it was over, Adam pulled her down close to him.

"I do love you, you know, Maggie."

"I know," she whispered. "I love you, too."

How easily they both lied, she thought.

It was a dreary day in mid-May and Maggie drove through the city, beside herself with excitement and sick with nerves; more petrified that Adam might spot her than anything else. She was relieved to leave the main roads behind and get onto the countryside route she had taken little more than three weeks before.

During the long journey her thoughts and feelings swung from confident and calm to terrified and panicked – and back again. By the time she arrived at Langley her nerves were in shreds and she felt mentally exhausted. She parked to the side of the manor and stood for a few moments looking up at the wooded hillside and breathing in deep breaths. The fresh air combined with the memories of that extraordinary place calmed her a little, but as she was led into the imposing house itself, she felt the last residue of confidence ebb away. Even the faces of the countless portraits hanging from the corridor walls seemed to be critically surveying her. It felt as though the interview had already begun.

She entered a small, dark room on the ground floor where she met the two people who were to interview her. The man, George Parkinson, was middle-aged and balding, with a round, pleasant face. He seemed an amiable man; the kind of person who puts others at ease without trying. He stepped forward without hesitation to shake her hand and even that action exuded warmth. He was accompanied by Geraldine Walker who, Maggie learned, would be her manager if she got the job.

In Maggie's eyes, this woman epitomised everything Maggie herself was not; elegant, professional, and supremely confident. She was possibly the most striking woman Maggie had ever seen, and as she did her best to answer the questions put to her, she became acutely aware of her own drab hair and unfashionable dress. All she could think of as she watched Geraldine observing her was *what on earth must she think of me?*

The interview progressed with straightforward questions Maggie could answer with reasonable ease, but she felt she was making little impact and fully expected the interviewers to have forgotten her within the hour.

"One more thing," Geraldine said, watching Maggie with inscrutable green eyes. "Why give up a job in a bank? You are far more likely to find chance of progression there than somewhere like this."

Maggie noted George Parkinson glance at Geraldine with a slight raising of his eyebrows.

"Oh, I wanted something different, something new. I suppose what I'm looking for is a fresh challenge in a new place. And what an amazing place this is." Maggie knew her answer sounded weak.

"Wanted a new challenge," Geraldine repeated, jotting down a note, and sounding far from convinced, as though she had heard that line once too often. She lifted her head and observed Maggie in total silence for a few disconcerting seconds. "You realise that working for me means hard work. This place may be pretty, but I have a successful business to run. And you think you are up to that?" Her tone was cool and measured with a hint of an accent Maggie had tried and failed to place throughout the interview.

Maggie's face flushed under the woman's gaze. Was this really the best she could do? This was a chance in a lifetime and she was allowing her fear and crippling lack of self-confidence to ruin everything. She steadied her voice.

"Yes, Mrs Walker, absolutely I do." She took a breath and looked at Mr Parkinson, reading the spark of a smile in his eyes that urged her on. "I have a wealth of experience in all kinds of administration and I think my knowledge of working with figures and cash will be a real asset to you. I know what it's like to work to deadlines, too. I'm not afraid of hard work – in fact I thrive on it."

"Anything else?" George Parkinson asked, as though encouraging her to continue.

He sees something in me, Maggie thought, *he wants me to do well.*

"You said that you have mostly manual, paper-based systems. Well, if ever you are interested in starting to use a computer, I have been using some of the latest PCs in the bank. I'm sure I could help develop some time-saving processes," she looked at Geraldine, "perhaps for your stocktake?"

"There you go, Geraldine," George Parkinson said brightly. "You've been saying how it's about time we caught up with technology."

"Hmm, we'll see about that." Geraldine stacked her papers, including Maggie's letter and reached for a larger pile to the side of the desk. "Thank you, Miss Armstrong, we will be in touch. We've had lots of applications as you can imagine."

As Maggie was led back through the manor, she prayed she'd done enough, but self-doubt haunted her. The faces of the portraits now seemed to view her with pity. She stood by her car searching for her keys and as she did so she heard a man's voice calling a name far off in the distance. She looked up to the wood and then south down to the parkland to where she knew the little cottage stood. There was no one in sight. Her skin prickled and she felt the goosepimples rise on her arms. She found her keys and quickly slipped into the car and drove away.

Maggie tried to carry on as normal – or as normal as could be now news that she was leaving had spread. She had always been guarded about her private life, and her unwillingness to mix (Adam didn't like her to socialise or have friends was nearer the truth) or engage in idle chit-chat had distanced her from colleagues. So when people she had barely spoken to came and wished her well, asking the inevitable questions about where she was going to, Maggie was uncomfortable in the extreme. She worried constantly that word would get out; that somehow Adam would discover her plan. After all, she had heard the gossip about him. She put people off by saying that she was waiting to finalise the formalities of her new job and preferred not to discuss it yet.

With only a week left before Maggie was due to leave the bank, she received a letter from Langley. Making an excuse to go to the bathroom, she locked herself into a cubicle and opened the letter. The envelope was stuck fast and her hands shook so much she struggled to open it. The letter was brief. It thanked Maggie for her time and went on to say that on this occasion her application had been unsuccessful. There was no further explanation.

Maggie sat down on the toilet seat staring at the letter in disbelief, feeling sick with disappointment. Her eyes fixed on the pale blue sheet headed *Langley Manor Estates*. What had she been thinking? What had made her believe, even for a second, that she would be good enough to work somewhere like that? The reality of what she'd done hit her like a physical blow and every ounce of resolve to make a fresh start vanished. It took a few minutes for her to compose herself sufficiently to go back to the counter, where she mechanically smiled and talked to customers with no memory of what she'd said to any of them.

Maggie was surprised to see Adam's car in the garage. He was seldom home before her. As she entered the kitchen the first thing she saw was her best handbag on the counter, the contents strewn about including her interview notification letter, which she had left in the bottom of the bag. Her heart seemed to stop and then leap back into action with a thud. The letter was still in its envelope.

"Adam?" she called nervously.

"In here." The voice sounded croaky.

He was laid out on the sofa with a blanket pulled over him.

Maggie's legs felt weak and she leaned against the door frame.

"Are you okay?"

"No, I've come down with a bloody cold. I couldn't find any tablets anywhere – might have known there'd be some in your bag. Remember to get some more when you go shopping."

Maggie steadied herself. "I'll put some out, they're in the cupboard. I'm just popping back to the car, I've forgotten something." Adam grunted in response.

Maggie snatched up the letter and hurried down to the basement where she tore it up along with the rejection letter and put them in the rubbish bin.

Heavy rain lashed down as people wearing long macs hurried along under umbrellas. Lights reflected on the wet pavement giving the impression of winter rather than late spring. Maggie sat at the bank counter staring absently out onto the street. The weather reflected how she felt. All that had been bright and warm and green had vanished. She hadn't slept the night before and she felt drained. With a huge effort, she smiled and chatted with customers and when there was a break in the queue, she contemplated asking if she could keep her job.

Janet, the supervisor, called to Maggie from a desk behind the counter. She was holding up a telephone receiver. "You know you're not supposed to receive private calls."

Maggie thanked her and ignored the rebuke. The switchboard operator put the call through, the voice on the end of the line sounding vaguely familiar.

"Maggie Armstrong?"

"Yes," Maggie replied.

"Geraldine Walker, Langley. Can you talk?"

Maggie's breath caught.

"Y... yes," she stammered.

Geraldine's voice was curt. "If you're still interested in the job here, I want to offer it to you. My first two choices let me down, so it's yours if you want it."

Maggie was stunned. She had gone from the depths of despair to the heights of elation in a matter of hours. The fact that she was Geraldine's third choice didn't register at all.

6

Gone

DURING THE MONTH THAT followed Maggie's decision to apply for the post at Langley, all her thoughts had been concentrated on getting the job. Now the practicalities of leaving and starting anew came into focus. She had agreed with Geraldine to start the new job the following Tuesday and now she only had four days to make arrangements. She decided that the best course of action was to contact Langley for advice. She phoned the manor house reception from a public phone box during lunch. Once the prim-sounding woman at the other end was satisfied who Maggie was, she gave her telephone numbers of places offering accommodation, which included the local pub, The Stag, and a few bed and breakfasts. The woman hinted that the Stag wouldn't be the best choice if Maggie wanted quiet and privacy. Maggie heeded her words and crossed it off her list. The last of three properties offering bed and breakfast sounded ideal. It was a farmhouse situated three miles from Langley, with a small self-contained, fully furnished annex. It had only recently come free and though it was more expensive than Maggie had planned, it sounded preferable to spending six months in a single room in someone's house. She made the arrangements and breathed a sigh of relief. All she had to do now was leave Adam and the nightmare would be behind her.

For Maggie, the weekend became nerve-shredding and endless. Despite his cold, Adam had been going to work, but on Saturday morning he announced he was feeling unwell and would be staying in. He loved to watch or play football and it was so unusual for him to stay at home on a Saturday that Maggie tortured herself with thoughts that somehow he had found out; that he had known her plans all along and was waiting to spring it upon her.

"It might do you good to get out in the fresh air, love," she said, trying to encourage him into his usual routine.

"Yes, well, it might do you good to just shut up. If you knew how I felt you wouldn't even suggest it."

Maggie retreated to the kitchen.

"I'll make some of your favourite soup for lunch. It might make you feel a bit better."

Adam didn't reply. Maggie chopped the vegetables and put a small chicken into the oven. She tried to clear her head. She had been relying on Adam being out of the flat at least some of the time over the weekend.

Adam stayed on the sofa, watching *Grandstand* on television. Maggie tidied the kitchen and then took two bowls of soup with brown bread to the dining table. Adam dragged himself to a chair, snuffling and coughing.

"I forgot to tell you, we're out on Wednesday night. We've been invited to John's place," he said.

John was a colleague of Adam; someone Maggie had heard of but had never met. It was unusual for her to be included with any of Adam's friends.

"Oh, that will be nice," Maggie said quietly, trying to keep the spoonful of soup heading for her mouth from shaking.

"Yes, well, try and make yourself look presentable for once, will you? You haven't a clue how unfashionable you look."

Maggie didn't need to be told. The last few years had been the age of big perms and shoulder pads – neither of which suited Maggie's short frame and fine, silky hair.

"I'll try," she said quietly, thinking, *I don't need to try ever again – I won't be here.* Then a thought came to her mind. "Actually, I was going to sort through my clothes and have a bit of a throw-out. I'll look out something suitable while I'm doing that. I'll be in the bedroom while you have a rest and watch TV."

Maggie put some of the belongings she planned to take into one black bin liner and the clothing she was throwing out into another. She kept some of her clothing neatly folded in her drawers and hanging in the wardrobe, ready to pack at the last minute.

"What are you throwing these out for?"

Adam had come into the room quietly and was now looking through the clothes she was taking with her. Maggie's mouth went dry.

47

"I thought about what you said. It's about time I got some new things. I thought I'd take those to a charity shop."

She kept her face turned away from him, convinced he would see through her; that he could read her mind. She folded a pair of jeans and made a point of placing them neatly in a drawer. She knew he was watching her. *He does know,* she thought, battling her nerves.

"Well, when you've finished you can sort some of my old stuff out as well – but make sure I get to see before you throw it."

Maggie listened to his feet padding back to the bathroom, and buried her face in an old sweater to muffle a sob of relief.

By Sunday Adam's cold had developed and he was feeling worse. He stayed in bed for most of the day and now Maggie had a new problem. What if he didn't go to work the next day? She lay awake for most of the night listening to Adam sneezing and coughing, as she tried to work out how to get her things out of the flat if he was still there. Eventually, she fell asleep with the comforting thought that compared to staying – leaving with nothing was perfectly acceptable.

The alarm jolted Maggie from the only deep sleep she'd had. It took her a second or two to remember what day it was, and then she waited, holding her breath to see if Adam responded. She bit her lip with anticipation when he dragged himself out of bed and with a few groans, started to dress for work. Maggie got up too, careful to carry out her usual routine; everything had to appear normal. They sat opposite each other at the breakfast bar, Maggie trying to force a slice of toast down, and Adam silently reading the newspaper. Then, with barely a glance in her direction, he got up, picked up his car keys and headed to the door.

"See you tonight," he said.

No you won't, Maggie thought.

"See you later," she said, convinced her voice was pitched higher than normal. "Hope you feel better."

Without responding, Adam closed the door behind him.

He doesn't know, Maggie thought, her body trembling with relief. *He has no idea — and now he's gone.*

One small suitcase, a bin bag and her bank book were all that Maggie needed to remove herself from Adam's life. She put her bags into the car and threw into the rubbish everything she didn't want. Then she went back to the flat and took one last look around. It was as though she had never been. Adam could bring someone back that evening and they would never know she had existed.

The only thing she had left to do was leave him a note. As much as she wanted to simply walk away without a word, it was important he understood that she had gone for good. She had to reduce the chance of him searching for her, or reporting her missing — though she thought that would be unlikely. Yes, he would be angry, feel betrayed, but he would soon be over that and then he would think of her as nothing more than a stray cat; something that had wandered into his life for a while and then moved on.

Maggie sat, her pen hovering over a sheet of lined paper. At last the words came in short, emotionless sentences:

Adam, I have left. I am starting a new life in the north. Don't try to find me. I have taken only my own things. I'm sure you won't miss me. I know about the affair. I don't care. I just hope you don't treat her as you have treated me. I'm sure you have already forgiven yourself for what you did. I will never forgive you.

That was all she put. She wanted to write page upon page about what her life had become, about how much he had hurt her; how he had damaged her; how much he had taken from her. But what was the point. All that mattered was that she did the thing she should have done long ago – leave.

7

The Petersons

HILLSIDE FARM WAS TUCKED away in a narrow valley three miles north of Langley and was run by Jack and Irene Peterson. Maggie pulled into the cobbled farmyard, which was enclosed on three sides by the house and an assortment of stone buildings.

Irene emerged from the house and hurried forward to greet Maggie. She looked nothing like Maggie had imagined. She had pictured a large, homely woman with a round, rosy face, wearing a flowery apron, but the woman who helped her with her few belongings was wiry and lean, and dressed in well-worn work shoes and overalls. She must have been around seventy years old, but she scuttled around at surprising speed on nimble legs. Her face was thin and lined, though not harsh. When she laughed, which was frequently, her face crinkled like scrunched paper and her bright eyes disappeared, engulfed by wrinkles. Her long grey hair was pinned up haphazardly with rogue strands that refused to stay in place, blowing in the breeze.

Maggie was shown into the single-storey stone annex attached at right angles to the left of the farmhouse and was deeply satisfied by what she found. The front door led into an open-plan room that contained a sleeping area, cosy living space by a log fire, and a sink, oven, small fridge, and a few cupboards in one corner. Two windows looked out onto the hillside to the rear of the building. The only other door, close to the bed, opened into a tiny, but surprisingly modern bathroom.

No sooner had they stepped through the door, than Irene began to fuss around making sure everything was just so; re-straightening the already tidy bed, and re-folding the beautifully neat towels.

"Now then, lovely, you just let me know if there is anything you need. I'll be assuming you want breakfast unless you tell me otherwise — it's at seven thirty every morning in the kitchen. And tonight you must join Jack and me for dinner."

It was the last thing Maggie felt like doing. She was so exhausted; not from the physical moving, but from the immense emotional tension of the past few days.

"Oh, no… really, Mrs Peterson, I don't want to intrude…"

"There's no question about it. You must be tired and you've got no food in yet." She smiled warmly at Maggie. "You get yourself settled and we'll see you at the house at six o'clock." With that, Irene straightened the folds of the floral curtains at the door window, and stepped back out into the cobbled yard. "You'll want to meet Jack anyway," she laughed. "See you later, lovely."

As Maggie closed the door, she knew two things; that she was more likely to be called 'lovely' than anything else – and that she liked Irene.

She unpacked her things and put her clothes into the small wardrobe. Then, finding fresh milk in the fridge, and tea, coffee and biscuits in a cupboard, she made a drink and, and even though it was only mid-afternoon, she lit the fire. She sat, staring into the growing flames, sipping her tea, and digesting what she had done. It was so hard to believe. Somewhere inside, she felt that soon she must return to the flat, back to Adam, and that this wonderful pretence would be over. Then she reminded herself she had really done it – she had made the break. There was no going back.

Maggie looked through her limited clothes and picked out a herringbone skirt and white blouse with lacy neck and cuffs. She was going to wear them for work, but she felt she needed to make more of an effort for dinner than her comfortable jeans and sweater. At six o'clock on the dot, she tapped on the farmhouse door. Irene opened it and immediately gushed forth a string of words that spilled out as quickly as she moved.

"Oh, come on in, lovely, come on in. Jack's not back yet, but I told him 'don't you be late for your dinner, Jack, as we've got a guest tonight', but that's Jack for you. He's always got this to do and that to do." Irene scuttled back to the large kitchen range and checked inside. The aroma of a meat pie emerged, and Maggie realised she was starving. "Anyway, come on, you come and sit in here and Jack won't be long." Irene ushered Maggie through into the adjoining lounge-cum-dining room, where a heavy oak table was set for three. The evening had grown cool and Maggie noticed that Irene had lit a fire, too.

The door opened and Jack Peterson entered, accompanied by several dogs. In stature, Jack and Irene could have been brother and sister. He, too, was small, but he looked muscular, with huge gnarled hands and arthritic knuckles. He spoke softly as he greeted Maggie without a smile or any accompanying niceties. She suspected the lines on his leathery face came from hard work and weather, rather than from laughing. The removal of his flat cap revealed a mostly bald head with a few long hairs on one side plastered strategically over the top. Maggie smiled inwardly; it was the poorest attempt at a 'comb over' she had seen.

Jack was followed by a variety of dogs; two black and white collies whose eyes never left their master, an old yellow Labrador who promptly flopped down in front of the fire, and a tall, thin greyhound-cross that looked peculiarly out of place.

"Jack, what have I said about bringing all the dogs in – especially when we've got visitors?" Irene said.

"Oh, be still, woman," said Jack, the words carrying no hint of annoyance or irritation. He settled himself in a chair by the fire, the two collies lying in front of him, watching. "They'll go back out in a minute."

"I should hope so, too." Irene looked at Maggie and nodded towards the collies. "Them's working dogs. That nearly white one's Gyp and the other one's Ted – there's no place for them in the house."

"Do they mind being outside?" Maggie asked. She knew little of dogs. She liked them – she liked all animals, but her family had never had pets and it had been out of the question in the city flat.

"Oh, they want to be outside," Irene said, fussing over finishing touches to the table. "They've got a cosy place in our barn – better than some folks' houses." She chuckled to herself. "I'm thinking of old Sam's place, Jack. He's an old lad lives up the valley on his own. I tell you, if our dogs went into his house they'd turn tail and head straight back to the barn. No question."

Maggie smiled. "What about the other two?" she asked, looking at the old Labrador, already fast asleep and the grey rough-haired lurcher who remained near the door, his long tail wagging in a low swing, like a pendulum.

"That Lab is Bess. She's a house dog, all right. Loves to go out on the farm with Jack, but likes her comforts when she gets back." Irene glanced across at the lurcher. "And that strange thing – well, we sort of inherited him, didn't we, Jack? A cousin of mine – a bit of an odd woman – had him and couldn't look after him when she became ill. Begged us to take him last year, didn't she, Jack?" Jack poked the fire and said nothing.

Maggie held a hand out to the dog. "What's his name?"

Irene chuckled. "Rupert – I tell you, what a name for a dog. But that's my cousin all over, isn't it, Jack? A bit, how would you put it? Eccentric – that's it, eccentric."

Maggie smiled as the dog sniffed her hand and then came forward to be stroked. "Hello, Rupert," she said, watching the tail swing quicker.

"Jack won't call him by his name, though – will you, Jack?" Jack said nothing. "No – he calls him Dog." She chortled again. "Just started to get used to his new name, he has."

Maggie listened, fascinated, by the one-sided conversation Irene had with her silent husband. It seemed that in Jack's presence she ran everything by him, without needing or expecting any kind of response.

The collies were eventually ejected and the Petersons and their new guest tucked into home-made meat and potato pie and fresh vegetables followed by apple crumble. After they had eaten, they sat together around the fire, and it was then that Irene's curiosity regarding this pale, frail-looking young woman finally got the better of her.

"So, what brings you here, all on your own then?"

Maggie knew the questions would come, but she didn't feel the same sense of intrusion from Irene that she had felt from others. Even so, she resolved to give away as little as possible. She gave a sparse summary of her reasons for moving and her words, though truthful, painted a different picture to reality because of what she chose not to say.

"I worked for a bank – it was the only job I've known and I was finding it so boring. And I hate being in the city – I've always wanted to live in the countryside, but I didn't think I'd ever be able to afford it. I just happened to see a job advertised at Langley Manor and it said there would be a cottage with it after a few months – so, here I am."

"Well, you're certainly in the countryside here, dear — miles from anywhere. Still, that's how we like it, isn't it, Jack?" Jack appeared to have nodded off, his chin resting on his chest. "This farm is rented from Langley Manor, you know? Well, of course you probably wouldn't know that. Oh yes, they own most of the property around here."

"No, I didn't know that, I don't know much about the place at all. Have you always worked this farm?"

"Yes, since we was married. Jack's father farmed it before him, and his grandad before that." Irene nodded at her husband. "Isn't that right, Jack?" Jack snored gently. She looked back at Maggie and deftly turned the conversation back to her guest.

"Anyway — what about you? Any family — parents? Husband?" Her eyes fell to Maggie's bare left hand. "Boyfriend, perhaps?"

"No, no family to speak of. Well, I have my father but… Well, we don't really have a great deal to do with each other." Maggie was surprised at how easily she found herself talking to Irene. She felt comfortable and welcome; even Rupert joined in, pushing his head under her hand for more attention.

"Oh dear, that is a shame. Any other close companions?" Irene continued, determined to get to the bottom of Maggie's marital, or otherwise, status.

"No… a long-term boyfriend, that's all. That's over now." Maggie smiled into Irene's kind eyes. "A bit of a new start, you might say." She hoped that Irene would get the hint that she didn't wish to say any more about the past, and that appeared to be the case.

"Well, I hope you enjoy staying with us until they get a house sorted for you."

"I'm sure I will, Mrs Peterson, and I can't thank you enough for making me feel so much at home." Maggie got to her feet, continuing to stroke the dog who now leaned his tall body against her legs. "And to Rupert, too," she laughed. "But I really should get settled in and try and get a good night's sleep – I need to be at my best for tomorrow."

"I should think you're feeling a bit nervous, aren't you?" Irene asked as they walked to the kitchen. "Moving today and starting your new job tomorrow – it's a lot to deal with."

Maggie had barely thought about the job. She had been so focused on today that the challenges of her new post had hardly occurred to her.

"Not really," she said, though the thought of joining Langley and the inevitable meeting of new people brought with it a familiar surge of anxiety. She took a deep breath to shake away the nerves and turned to Irene, a bright smile lighting her face. "Like I said, this is a new start, and I suppose I'm excited more than anything."

Maggie said goodnight and stepped out into the light spring evening. The blackbirds were starting their evening chorus against a background of distant bleating lambs. She closed her eyes and pictured the sights and sounds of the city that were ingrained into her mind. She imagined she was back there and that this was all a dream. Then she opened her eyes again and gazed across the green rolling hills and breathed in the clear country air. She smiled to herself and wondered if she could dare to be happy. It felt an age since she'd said goodbye to Adam for the last time. He would be home now, and she could picture him standing in the stark apartment, reading her note, shaking with anger. Simply the knowledge that she'd had the courage to take matters into her own hands and leave him would be enough to enrage him. She felt the fear rise in the pit of her stomach and then, a second later, it faded. He couldn't hurt her today; not any day. In the space of twelve hours, her life had changed forever.

As Maggie climbed into bed and soon drifted off into a deep and dreamless sleep, her final thought was, *please don't let this be too good to be true.*

8

Keeper's Cottage

MAGGIE DROVE THE SHORT distance to Langley Manor, her stomach churning with a combination of nerves and excitement.

At the arched gateway to the manor, she was met by Pamela Collins. Pamela was a middle-aged woman with short grey hair and a serious expression. She greeted Maggie with efficiency more than warmth.

"Good morning, Margaret Armstrong? I'm Pamela – you can call me Pam."

Maggie shook her hand, aware that her own was cold and clammy. She took a deep breath and tried to appear relaxed and confident.

"Hello, Pam, it's lovely to meet you – please call me Maggie. I'm so excited to be working here."

Pam observed Maggie queerly for a moment as though she didn't understand why anyone would be excited by the prospect of working there. "Well, let me show you to where you'll be working," she said, a little stiffly. "You will share an office with me for some of the week. I'm only here two days — you'll have it to yourself the rest of the time."

Maggie followed Pam through the gateway where a security man, standing in a small stone room to the left, nodded a good morning. They continued in silence along a gravel drive towards huge studded doors that opened into the manor. They walked at a steady pace, and Maggie soon realised this was top speed for Pam who was already breathing hard and seemed reluctant to combine conversation with exercise. Maggie didn't mind, it gave her chance to take in her surroundings.

She was proud to be working inside the manor house, and as they walked she concentrated hard, trying to remember every door they entered and each turn they took through the maze of corridors. But she was so awed by the ancient building that she soon forgot where she was or how she'd got there.

In between applying for the post and getting the job, Maggie had read up all she could about Langley. As far as historic houses went, the manor wouldn't be considered large, but it was one of the best examples of medieval houses in England. Parts had been altered inside over the centuries; changes that had made the house more comfortable to live in, but externally it looked very much as it had in the early1400s, and inside it still retained its impressive original great hall and kitchens.

Irene had given Maggie a crumpled copy of a guidebook sold to visitors to the gardens and she had read as much as she could over breakfast. The guide gave more interesting information about the estate, beyond its ancient history.

Despite the modest size of the building, Langley had retained extensive land and property. The park and woodland covered almost 3,000 acres, and surrounding that was a further 25,000 acres farmed by tenants. There were more than 200 properties in the immediate area belonging to the estate, ranging from small cottages to grand detached houses, farms and crofts of varying sizes, and even an old coaching inn. The Stag Inn was situated on the road through the nearby village of Bransby. The village, which sat just outside the western boundary of the park, belonged entirely to Langley with many of the cottages housing employees.

The estate had been in the Handley family for almost 200 years, the current owner being Richard Handley. Only the manor gardens were open to the public, although Richard had made a minor break in tradition by allowing visitors into the old kitchens, which had recently become a tea room.

Pam led the way through the great hall, with its high beamed ceiling and tapestry-draped walls, and Maggie hung back, marvelling at a space that had changed little in 600 years. The hall was utterly silent except for the rhythmic tick of a grandfather clock. With no other furniture in the room, the clock stood alone in a corner and looked lonely and out of place. Maggie closed her eyes, and breathed in the unique scent. The smell was difficult to define; she could detect a hint of wood and beeswax polish, but to Maggie it just smelt old. Not the smell of decay, but that of lives lived, or periods long gone — it was the scent of time. Remembering the fumes and clamouring noise of the city, she wanted to shout for joy.

At the far end of the hall Pam opened a door with an exaggerated rattle that Maggie took as a hint to hurry along. A creaking staircase took them up three floors and into what must have been the original attic rooms, several of which had been turned into offices. The room that Maggie would share with Pam was unexpectedly large with two leaded windows, low to the floor and looking out onto the front of the manor towards the river and bridge. The ruined south wing stood forlornly off to the left.

The office was kitted out with modern desks and cabinets. Maggie noticed an unused computer pushed into one corner, its box still under the table along with a thick instruction book. The walls were painted pale cream, brightened further by harsh fluorescent strip lights along the ceiling, and the brown, hard-wearing carpet reminded her of the flooring in the bank. In fact, were it not for the sloping walls, and deep-set windows, it could have been an office anywhere.

Two further doors opened from the room. One led to a small kitchenette, the other Pam pushed open with a flourish and beckoned Maggie forward to look.

"This is Mrs Walker's office," Pam said formally. "She doesn't like anyone going in when she's not here, but she won't mind me showing you."

Maggie stepped forward, feeling as though she was entering a sacrosanct part of the building. The room was impressive. It faced the same direction as the adjoining office, but was longer. The walls were painted in rich crimson, with white ceiling and skirting and the walls were adorned with original oil paintings. A huge leather-topped desk stood near the windows and leather chairs were strategically placed around the room for guests. An impressive woven rug of pinks and greens covered the majority of the floor with polished wood showing neatly around the edges. The warm glow from brass lights around the walls gave the room a soothing feel. If it wasn't for the fact that Maggie knew whose office it was, it might easily be mistaken as the plush study of the owner of the manor.

Maggie was a little relieved to discover that Geraldine was away on business and wouldn't be back until the following week. She felt glad of the chance to find her feet before having to work with her new manager.

The first day flew by quickly as Pam showed Maggie the basics of the tasks she would be doing. Most of it seemed straightforward and Maggie was confident she would soon get the hang of her duties. Pam was virtually silent other than when showing Maggie what she had to do and pointing out where things were. All Maggie managed to get from her was that she had worked at Langley for several years and had been a part-time secretary to Richard Handley's father in his last years. Since his death, Pam had been content to work two days each week for Geraldine and take the winter off when the place was closed to the public. Her clipped responses to further questions told Maggie not to expect much in the way of conversation.

At five o'clock Maggie's first work day at the manor ended and, with hours of light left, she changed into her walking shoes and set off up into the wood. The thought had come to her that morning – what better way to end her first day at Langley than to return to the spot that had made such a powerful impression on her.

The wood had been transformed. When she had visited, only a few weeks before, many of the trees had still been in bud. Now the foliage was thick and green, and the parkland down below completely hidden. When the giant oak came into view, Maggie chuckled to herself. She had half expected it not to be there. The events of that strange Friday morning seemed so much like a dream she sometimes wondered if it had happened at all. She had been in such a dreadful state; she was convinced she was ill. But there the tree stood in all its majesty, and now cloaked in fresh green it looked more impressive than ever.

She rested her hand on the trunk; half scared, half hoping to experience that inexplicable rush of emotion again. There was nothing – simply the sounds of the countryside on an early summer afternoon, and the voices she heard this time were those of visitors to the park, drifting up from the valley below.

Maggie sat down on the flat stone and resting her chin on her hands, she looked out from the rocky edge across the park. The last time she'd sat there, she had known her life would change, but she could never have imagined that fate would bring her back to this very place.

Down below she could make out the lonely cottage, standing above the reed beds north of the manor. As she gazed across the landscape, her eye was constantly drawn back to it, sitting as it did like an island hemmed in by the marsh and river to two sides and the parkland to the north and east. As she shielded her eyes from the sun, trying to bring the little building into clearer focus, she was overcome by the urge to go down to it.

She jogged back down the steep track to the manor and then ran along the road that led into the north park. She felt physically stronger and more energised than she'd felt in years and just half an hour after leaving the flat stone at the top of the hill, Maggie was standing before Keeper's Cottage. The curious building looked like a kind of gatehouse, although she couldn't quite see why it would be, positioned as it was, seemingly in the middle of nowhere. It was small and oddly shaped; built from honey-coloured stone and looking distinctly different to many of the cottages in the nearby village. It had large sash windows, instead of the more common leaded panes, and they looked out across the park. From what she could see, there were bits of additions built onto it here and there, as if whoever had designed it had no clear idea of what they wanted. To the rear, a section of the park had been fenced in by metal railings to create a garden. The unmade road she had followed from the manor ran on past the cottage, at which point the surface disappeared beneath a layer of grass. The green track that remained continued in the direction of the river. A footpath leading walkers from the bridge by the manor along the edge of the marsh and into the north end of the park passed in front of the cottage just a few feet from the windows.

Maggie gazed at the building, sensing a desire beyond inquisitiveness, to go inside. As she hesitated by the gate, wondering if she dared knock at the door, a strange stillness developed around her. The natural sounds, the breeze, the birds, the sheep and cattle, all fell silent, and she felt her skin prickle.

"Mary!"

A man's voice called out.

Maggie was startled. She started to move away, rubbing at the goosepimples that had risen on her arms.

"Mary!" The man's voice called again from somewhere to the back of the cottage.

Maggie couldn't resist looking into the neglected garden. Untrimmed bushes and shrubs encroached on the roughly cut grass, and a yew tree, damaged by wind, leaned precariously at the edge of the lawn. There was no person in sight.

"MARY!" The voice called for a third time, closer now and with more urgency. As she looked around, the voice stirred a memory in Maggie's mind. She was sure it must belong to one of the many people she'd heard speak during the day, but she could see no one. Maggie waited in the stillness, hoping – wanting – to see who spoke. At that moment, the cottage door opened and as it did, the songs of the birds and the bleating of sheep returned. She could feel the breeze once more on her face as the strange atmosphere lifted.

A young, fair-haired man stepped out from the cottage.

"Are you lost?" he asked.

"Oh, hmm, no." Maggie cringed. "I'm so sorry if you think I was being nosey. I work here you see — I'm new — well, actually, this is my first day."

The man's smile broadened and he came over to the gate. Maggie couldn't tell if he was being friendly or just finding humour in her discomfort.

"Mark Thompson — trainee land agent," he said, reaching through the railings to shake Maggie's hand.

"I'm Maggie Armstrong — and please, don't let me interrupt your evening."

"Not at all. I hope you enjoy working here. What are you going to be doing?"

"Oh, just administration for the garden centre and the restaurant. I'm working for Geraldine Walker."

Mark's expression changed. For the briefest moment the smile diminished. "Well, I'm sure you'll find it a great place to work. What brings you down to my end of the park — I charge an entrance fee, you know?" The grin returned.

Maggie laughed. She decided he was friendly. "I was interested to see who lives here." She pointed over her shoulder to the wood. "I first saw the cottage from up there and thought what a great place it is."

"Well, I've lived here for a year and a bit, but hoping to move on at some point. Got to get the career going — you know, 'onwards and upwards' as they say."

"Won't you be able to stay on here?" Maggie asked, incredulous that anyone would want to leave.

"No, that's not likely. It's a bit of a tradition here. They take on a young bloke from college as a trainee, and then after a year you're expected to go off into the big wide world and get a proper job somewhere. I think I'm probably outstaying my welcome." He laughed, not seeming to care if his employer had noticed his tardiness or not. Maggie smiled and wondered what it must be like to be so carefree.

"I bet you won't find anywhere to live as unusual as this."

"Oh, it's nice enough, but a bit out in the sticks... and too far from the pub."

"I heard someone calling – just now – it was a man calling 'Mary'. Was that you?"

"No," Mark replied, "it wasn't me. And no one called Mary living here either – more's the pity." He flashed a cheeky smile and Maggie flushed. "Anyway, there doesn't seem to be anyone around," he said, looking up and down the deserted footpath.

"Oh, I must have been mistaken," Maggie said, knowing that another person was in the vicinity, somewhere.

"Why don't you come in for a coffee, and I can tell you a bit about the place?" Mark said, clicking down the latch on the gate and opening it towards him.

"No." The word shot out before she could stop it and Maggie was aware that she sounded rude. "Sorry... what I mean is I've got to get back for dinner. I'm staying with the Petersons... you know, up the valley, and I'm dining with them this evening."

"Ok, well, maybe next time," Mark said, without showing the slightest sign of offence.

"Thanks for the offer. Perhaps I'll see you around."

"Hope so." He waved cheerily and disappeared back inside.

Maggie walked away, looking back over her shoulder every few strides. She kicked herself for not accepting Mark's offer and missing the chance to look inside the cottage. The real reason for declining nagged at her and was impossible to ignore; she couldn't bear the thought of being alone with a man. And she couldn't imagine that feeling ever going away.

By the time she reached her car, the memory of the man calling the woman's name had slipped from her mind.

9

The Stag Inn

Pam wasn't in and Maggie had arrived at the office half an hour early, determined to make a good impression. Despite her intentions, the old building and the view from her window were a constant distraction. She found her eyes lifting from the paperwork and gazing out, past the cedar trees to the shimmering river and parkland beyond. She had to keep reminding herself of where she was, of what she had done, as though at any moment the view would vanish and be replaced by the crowded streets of the city. For a moment she was transported back, standing by the busy road she crossed each morning, the blaring of car horns in her ears, the smell of exhaust fumes in her nose. Her heart thumped as she pictured Adam waiting on the opposite side of the road, his grey eyes staring at her.

The sound of high heels on floorboards in the corridor interrupted Maggie's thoughts and a moment later the door was thrust open and Geraldine Walker breezed in.

Even though Maggie had met her before, she was struck again by Geraldine's appearance. It wasn't that she was classically beautiful, more that her looks and the way she carried herself were so striking. She was tall; Maggie guessed at least five feet ten, lithe and slim – almost thin. She was immaculately and expensively dressed in an emerald-green designer suit, the modest shoulder pads further accentuating her waist. She exuded such an air of confidence and authority that her presence alone compelled Maggie to jump to her feet.

"Hello, Mrs Walker, it's so nice to meet you again."

Maggie stepped forward, extending her hand. Geraldine hesitated, waiting for Maggie to come to her. Her expression conveyed mild irritation at finding a new person in the office – as though she had forgotten Maggie would be there.

"Yes, of course," Geraldine said, as if in answer to her own thoughts.

She raised a hand. Her wrist was bedecked in a heavy gold charm bracelet, which jangled and flashed expensively during the perfunctory handshake. Geraldine remained motionless, regarding her new assistant silently. Her angular features were only slightly softened by her wide mouth and full lips. Her smooth skin was pale and flawless. Maggie had no idea how old she was, but guessed she must be in her late thirties, though fine lines around her mouth suggested she could be older. Her green, cat-like eyes were remarkable, with perfectly applied make-up enhancing them further. Finally, her face was framed by thick shoulder-length hair of an extraordinarily vibrant copper colour.

Maggie had been intimidated by Geraldine at the interview, but had put that down to nothing more than her own nerves. Now, as the green eyes surveyed her for what seemed like endless seconds, she wasn't so sure. Maggie felt as though she was shrinking under the woman's gaze; becoming smaller and dowdier by the second. When Geraldine spoke, it was in the same cool tones, carrying the trace of unfamiliar accent that Maggie remembered.

"Get me a coffee, will you – white, no sugar? And make it strong." Geraldine turned towards her own adjoining office, and then looked back over her shoulder. "That's what I want each morning when I get in – I don't expect to have to ask. Oh, and you can call me Geraldine."

Maggie made the drink as quickly as she could and then hesitated by the door to steady the tremble in her hand. When she entered, Geraldine was seated behind the desk, telephone in hand.

"George, I don't care what the authorities are saying now. They reported that the building work could be done and it's been done. I am not holding up my business for a bunch of bureaucrats who've got nothing better to do than waste my time." She motioned for Maggie to put the coffee down and still listening to the person on the other end of the line, shook a cigarette from its box. The bracelet charms clinked. "Oh, for God's sake, George, stand up to these people." She put the cigarette to her lips. "You're the Langley agent for crying out loud. I will not lose money by closing the restaurant, not even for one day – get it sorted."

In an instant it seemed to Maggie that the warmth and calm she'd felt in that room the week before was sucked from it. She turned away and hurried back to her own office and closed the door. Was that George Parkinson that Geraldine had been speaking to? Maggie felt her stomach flip.

During the following few weeks, Maggie kept her head down and concentrated on her work. Despite having been recruited as Geraldine Walker's assistant, she had little contact with her; in fact it wasn't unusual for Geraldine to leave or return to the office without acknowledging Maggie at all. When Geraldine was next door, Maggie found herself in an almost constant state of tension. Not the horrible fear induced by Adam, but tightness in her muscles, as though on constant alert, that only lifted when Geraldine left. She also noticed that when Pam was at work, she was quieter than ever if Geraldine was around and seldom spoke unless work demanded it. From time to time, Maggie was required to go to the garden centre to check queries on deliveries. The newly expanded centre was impressive, built into the original stable block with a large shop and restaurant inside as well as an outside area for plants and garden furniture. Maggie relished these brief respites from the office, though Pam warned her that Geraldine would not take kindly to her missing for any length of time.

Maggie's only other legitimate escape from her attic room, was to drive across the park to Bransby House, a large building now used as the main offices for the estate. Bransby House stood next to the Stag Inn on the main road through the village. Amongst others, George Parkinson and the accounts team were based there and Maggie was required to take the week's invoices each Friday.

On her fourth Friday, Maggie entered the first-floor office and recognised two of the women from previous weeks. They had been pleasant enough without showing any particular interest in the newcomer. The third lady, who Maggie hadn't seen before, was very different. She got up from her desk and came across the room, her face beaming.

"Hello, Maggie isn't it? It's great to meet you, I'm Anne."

Anne was in her forties and wearing a formal navy suit. She had black, curly hair and a rosy complexion.

"How are you finding the place? Is everyone helping you to settle in?"

"Everyone's been so helpful, thanks," Maggie said, trying to keep images of Geraldine from her mind. "It's just quite hard to get to know people when you're stuck in your office all day. Not that I don't enjoy being in the manor – it's wonderful, but up in the attic, you seldom see anyone."

"That's one advantage of being over here," said Anne. "People from across the estate are always popping in for one thing or another. I tell you what, why don't you meet me after work at the Stag? We can have a quick drink and a chat – perhaps introduce you to one or two people. There's usually quite a few who drop in on a Friday on the way home."

Maggie hesitated. She had promised herself from day one that she would fight her shyness and get to know people, and perhaps even let them get to know her. She was annoyed at herself for failing at the first hurdle with Mark Thompson.

"Thank you. That would be good — it's very kind of you."

"Not at all. I'll see you shortly after five. Grab a table if you get there before me." She nodded her head towards her colleagues. "I'm sure you've already met Charlotte and Denise, haven't you?"

"Yes, although we were never introduced properly," Maggie said, thinking they hadn't exactly gone out of their way to make her feel welcome. Now, as though taking Anne's lead, they appeared friendlier and came over to shake her hand.

"We'll call in, too, if that's okay," Denise offered.

"There you go, that's decided then. We'll see you later," said Anne.

As well as being a traditional hostelry for locals and visitors alike, the Stag also doubled as a kind of social club for Langley workers. It was a place where everybody knew everyone else and it was somewhere Maggie would normally have avoided.

The interior of the bar was dark and the air was thick with cigarette smoke and the smell of beer. Maggie was astounded at the number of people standing at the bar or seated at the scattered tables. She searched through the gloom for Anne and unable to see her, ordered a soft drink and retreated to a table in an even darker corner of the room.

The inn appeared to be as ancient as the manor. The beamed ceiling and walls sloped at strange angles, and the stone-flagged floor was worn by centuries of footfall. Around the walls hung framed photographs of the inn and the manor, some going back to the 1800s. One, close to where Maggie sat, showed a team of horses being unhitched from a coach outside the inn. She stood to take a closer look. The horses were steaming, one tossing its head so that the image blurred. A young stable hand was unfastening the harnesses and, resting against the wall of the inn, a man stood watching, pipe in his mouth. He stood by the window Maggie could see now across the room. It fascinated her to think how a building could remain the same whilst everything and everyone around it changed with the passing years.

A waft of smoke drifted by and for a second it was as though the image she was viewing had come to life. The smell of the tobacco brought a childhood memory back to Maggie; vivid and yet elusive. She turned to see an elderly man sitting at the next table, drawing on a freshly lit pipe. He nodded a silent 'hello' in Maggie's direction. Maggie forced a smile and nodded back, but there was something about the room that cast a strange feeling over her. The stone flags, the tobacco, and the smell of beer... something familiar and yet disturbing. Maggie shivered as the grey smoke from the man's pipe curled towards her and the peculiar feeling intensified. With it came the sudden urge to run outside, but just as she moved from behind the table, a voice called loudly from across the room.

"There she is. Hey, Maggie."

The two women from the accounts office eased through the throng, and positioned themselves either side of Maggie, forcing her to sit back down.

"Anne's been held up, she'll be here in a minute," Denise said. "We'll get you another drink then you can tell us a bit about yourself; we've not had a chance to talk."

The arrival of the two women dispelled the weird atmosphere and Maggie settled back, for once relieved for the company. The two women had clearly run a comb through their hair and carefully reapplied heavy make-up and dark lipstick. Maggie could visualise her own pale face. She couldn't remember the last time she'd put on lipstick.

"Not much to tell I'm afraid," Maggie said, looking down and swilling her drink around her glass. "Actually, I think you will find me quite boring. I was looking for a new start and thought this would be an ideal place."

"Somebody said you've moved from the city – why would you want to do a thing like that and end up out here in the sticks?" Charlotte asked.

"Town life never suited me, even though that's all I've ever known. I think I'm a country girl at heart." Maggie glanced hopefully in the direction of the door, but there was still no sign of Anne.

"What about husband, boyfriend – are you on your own?" Denise said, her eyes scanning Maggie's left hand, just as Irene's had.

The questions were inevitable and Maggie was halfway through her well-practised reply when she saw Anne waving and making her way towards them.

"Don't listen too much to these two," Anne said. "They might appear harmless, but you won't find two worse gossips anywhere on the estate."

"Ooh, Anne, how can you say that?" Denise said, taking mock offence. "You know we only pass on information that is factual and verified."

Anne laughed out loud. "Oh yes, I'm sure."

Following close behind Anne was George Parkinson. Maggie caught his eye, and then looked away embarrassed. It didn't put him off.

"Nice to see you again – Maggie, isn't it?"

"That's right, Mr Parkinson."

He pulled a spare chair over from the next table and sat down. Maggie noticed Charlotte and Denise catching each other's eye.

"How have you been getting on?" George said to Maggie.

"Fine, thank you. Pam has shown me the ropes – I think I'm getting to grips with everything."

"Good. And I understand you're staying at Jack Peterson's place. He and Irene are a good sort. You'll be fine there until we get you sorted with a place of your own."

"Oh, they're very friendly. Well – Irene is; Jack doesn't say much. But I'm really comfortable there."

George threw his head back chuckling, the dim light from the lamps reflecting on his bald head.

"Yes – that's old Jack, a man of few words, but a heart of gold. His family have farmed on the estate for centuries. Anyway, I'll let you know when something suitable comes up for you."

"Thank you, Mr Parkinson. But I realise that won't be for at least six months?"

He moved a little closer and lowered his voice. Denise and Charlotte leaned in too.

"That's what we say. But once someone has settled into the job and looks as though they are here to stay – well, if the right place comes available, it makes sense to get them settled in. Better that than leaving properties standing empty." He looked away and caught the attention of a man across the room. "There's someone I need to speak to. It's good to see you, Maggie, I'll keep in touch."

"Thank you very much," Maggie called after him.

"Well, you're honoured," Denise said in hushed tones. "He's the land agent – looks after all the properties." Maggie nodded. This was not news to her. "You know that after Richard Handley, George Parkinson is the most important person here?"

That was something Maggie hadn't realised. It certainly hadn't seemed like that at the interview, and it made the way Geraldine had spoken to him on the telephone even more shocking.

"So, how do you like working for Geraldine Walker?" asked Charlotte, as though reading Maggie's mind.

"Oh, fine, thanks. To tell the truth I don't see that much of her."

"Well, that's good," said Charlotte, raising an eyebrow to Denise, "because by all accounts she can be, how can I put it...?"

"Bloody horrible," Denise chimed in, nudging Charlotte. They both giggled.

"I don't think there's need for that," Anne scolded and changed the subject. "Have you met the Handleys yet, Maggie?"

"No, not yet. I understand they go away for a few weeks at this time of year."

"That's right. Once the place is open for the new season, they take themselves off for a break, but they're quite hands-on the rest of the time – well, Richard is. I think Christina loves the new garden shop, but she leaves the running of things to Geraldine."

"She's very kind, Christina," Charlotte said. "You'll like her. Richard's a bit scary, though."

"Yes, 'small-man syndrome', if you ask me," Denise added.

"He's just a good businessman, that's all," said Anne. "I think they're both good people to work for."

As the conversation progressed, Denise and Charlotte realised that juicy gossip would not be forthcoming and soon left. Anne stayed on and chatted to Maggie, telling her about herself, but never prying into Maggie's life and leaving her to say as little or as much as she wanted. Maggie became so relaxed in Anne's company that she found herself engaged in conversation in a way she had seldom been before. She talked about her job at the bank, the move to Langley and life with Irene and Jack. Anne in turn introduced her to several people who came into the inn and before she knew it an hour had flown by.

"Thank you for this evening," Maggie said, picking up her bag and making a move to leave. "I've enjoyed myself more than I expected to."

"Not much of a socialiser, then?" There was no criticism in Anne's voice.

"No." Maggie looked away. "I suppose I like my own company."

"And there's nothing wrong with that."

The two of them made their way out to the car park, and Maggie took the chance to say something that had been niggling at her.

"Anne, can I ask you – is Geraldine as bad as they said? Only… I have to admit, I find her a bit intimidating."

Anne looked in the direction of the manor for a second or two, as though trying to decide what to say. In the end she smiled cheerfully at Maggie and placed a hand on her arm.

"You know what? I'm a big fan of taking people as you find them. Some people don't get along with Geraldine, but that doesn't mean you won't. And this is the best way to start – with a clean sheet. You get to know her first before listening to what others have to say."

"Thank you for the reassurance. I'd like to meet up with you again, to find more out about the place. Pam doesn't say much and I want to try and understand more about how Langley works."

"Of course. I tell you what, why don't you come over one weekend for lunch and meet by husband, Tom? We can have a good natter then."

Maggie drove back into the farmyard, to be greeted by a joyous Rupert who raced to her, tail wagging frantically. As she patted him and waved to Irene through the kitchen window, Maggie felt a glow of contentment. It was as though she had found a family. Irene was warm and generous, and Jack exuded kindness in his silent way; even Rupert had taken a shine to her. And now there was Anne, who was witty and kind and self-assured. She radiated a positive quality to which Maggie felt a spontaneous attachment.

The sound of men's voices, chatting and laughing, crept upon her. The smell of tobacco smoke invaded her nose and she could hear the scraping of booted feet dragging across the stone-flagged floor. She peered through the crowd of tall men, looking up at their faces, indistinct in the dim light. She was searching for someone. Then panic enveloped her as she realised she'd left something behind and ran back, tripping and stumbling over the uneven floor to the wooden bench. There the tiny carved horse lay. With relief she snatched it up and put it into her pocket.

Maggie sat bolt upright in bed and swung her feet onto the soft carpet. The sound was gone and the air in the room was fresh and clean. She felt to her side. There was no pocket. There was no wooden horse. After a few minutes she settled back down, but two hours passed before sleep finally returned.

10

The Offer

MAGGIE AND ANNE SAT together on the patio, soaking up the evening sunshine. It was warm and humid after a blistering day, but now the lightest breath of breeze made the temperature pleasant.

Anne's husband, Tom, stood by the open French windows. Maggie had been wary of him at first. He was intelligent and serious, and the fact that he was a solicitor had made her irrationally intimidated. But, as they had chatted over lunch, she had relaxed in the company of a kind and astute man.

"I'll leave you ladies to have a good chat, but first I think you need a wine refill." Tom disappeared inside.

"He's very friendly," Maggie said. "In a serious way, if you know what I mean."

"I do know what you mean," Anne said. "To tell you the truth, he was so serious I thought he was a little grumpy when I first met him. But he's got a great sense of humour – you just have to dig for it a bit."

"And I can't believe you're grandparents – I've never seen anyone who looks as young and glamorous as you and actually has a grandchild."

"Is that me you're talking about?" said Tom, reappearing with wine bottle in hand.

"Oh, look, there's that sense of humour I was telling you about," Anne said and Tom leaned over and gave her a quick kiss. Maggie smiled at the gentle show of affection.

Tom left and Anne continued. "We got married very young and had James soon after. Life wasn't easy in those first years and I think we missed out on so much, being tied down at such a young age. We were disappointed when James did exactly the same thing. We tried to dissuade him, but I think that made him more determined, and off he went at twenty and settled down with a girl."

A flush came to Maggie's cheeks. That had been her – everything she had longed for. She had tried so hard to make it work and had ended up with nothing. No husband and no baby. Tears burned behind her eyes and she coughed to swallow the lump in her throat. She pretended it was the wine.

"Is he happy?"

"Very. You know, despite our fears, it was the best thing that ever happened to him. He's such a great dad and his wife, Jenny... I know it's a cliché, but she is like a daughter."

Maggie enjoyed the way Anne talked about her family and their lives. She was a contented woman who had found her place in life. That was what Maggie wanted now – if she could get to be even a little bit like Anne, she would be happy. But even as the thought flitted through her mind, the hidden pain deep within reminded her that ultimate contentment was a goal that could never be reached.

"So how's it going?" Anne asked, refilling the glasses.

It had taken longer than expected to get together at Anne's house and five weeks had passed since their first meeting at the Stag. Up until now, in the company of Tom, they had avoided talking about work.

"It's great," Maggie said. "I could never have imagined that I'd end up working somewhere like this. I'm so lucky." Her face betrayed her positive words.

"I sense a 'but'."

"You can guess what the 'but' is," said Maggie, worry lines appearing on her brow. "Sometimes I think it must be me. I just need to toughen up."

"Has she done anything in particular?" They both knew who they were talking about without speaking her name.

"No, that's what's frustrating. If I told you exactly what she'd said, you would wonder what I was moaning about. It's more about her tone and the expression on her face." Maggie sat back and looked up at the sky as though searching for answers. "I actually think she really dislikes me."

"What makes you say that? You're good at what you do, you don't cause her any problems – what is there to dislike?"

"I don't know. I could imagine Geraldine being hostile towards someone who might threaten her, but I must be the least threatening person she's ever worked with. I don't know what to do to get her to like me or at least respect me."

Anne raised her eyebrows, pushing a dark curl of hair behind her ear. "Do you think Geraldine likes or respects anyone?"

"Probably not – apart from Mr Handley; he's the only person I've heard her be civil with. Even Mrs Handley seems to avoid her."

"Have you met the Handleys then?"

"I've seen them briefly, but not to talk to. Geraldine didn't introduce me – I don't think they know who I am." Maggie sighed. "Why do people have to be so difficult?"

"Well, some people seem to be put on this earth for one thing – to make others feel miserable," Anne said, nodding in agreement.

"I know, but I promised myself I wouldn't let it happen again."

Anne looked at Maggie; a silent question hung in the air as a cooling breeze rippled between them.

"Oh, take no notice of me." Maggie was acutely aware of her slip and tried to sound brighter. "To tell you the truth, I don't see that much of Geraldine, so I should be grateful. She's often out at meetings and when she is in, she doesn't talk to me much." She glanced at Anne whose eyes were still searching hers. "I'll get used to her, and anyway, I think a lot of this is down to me – that's one of my problems, I think too much."

They sat in silence for a minute watching the swallows swooping low to snatch insects from the humid air; one pair returning again and again to a mud nest clinging under the eaves of the house.

"Do you know much about Geraldine's background?" Maggie asked. "Pam doesn't talk about her at all and there's no way Geraldine would tell me anything about herself."

"I've pieced bits together about her from various people since I've been here. You know Geraldine works directly for Richard and Christina Handley. Anyway, when Richard started to develop the place – he inherited Langley about four years ago – one of the first things he did was look for a business manager. George Parkinson was experienced when it came to running the country estate and properties, but I think Richard wanted someone with a commercial background to get his new projects off the ground. Apparently he advertised the job in the national press and was amazed when he got an application from this high-flying business woman in Canada."

"Ah, that explains the accent – but she's not Canadian, is she?"

"No, British, but she'd been working out there for years. No one seems to know exactly what she did, but some say she's worked for several companies from different sectors – 'rescuing' some that were in difficulty, and getting others off the ground. Word has it that her experience was way beyond what Mr Handley had expected to attract and that they couldn't afford her."

"So how come she's here?"

"They negotiated a salary – still beyond what they'd planned to pay, but also offered her a superb house, on the estate."

"Where does she live?" It occurred to Maggie that although she knew Geraldine lived in the village, she had no idea in which house, and she wouldn't have dreamt of asking her directly.

"Almost next door to the Stag, Bransby Manor, the building on the opposite side to the estate office."

Maggie was vaguely aware that there was a large house hidden by a high wall on the edge of the village. She chuckled. "I might have known that she lives in a *manor*. But did she come back all the way from Canada for this job?"

"No, we think she met an Englishman out there – he's now her husband; a barrister. His name's Alan. Tom sees him from time to time in court – says he seems a decent sort of chap. They've got four children between them; two each from previous marriages."

Maggie couldn't begin to imagine what it would be like being married to Geraldine. But even harder to picture was Geraldine as a mother.

"Anyway, cutting a long story short," Anne continued, "some of which I don't know for certain, Geraldine was put in charge of the new parts of the business; she recruited specialists – you know, chefs, gardeners and the like, to run the individual departments, but she's ultimately responsible for it."

"It still seems a small business for her," Maggie said, imagining Geraldine's former life as a city trouble-shooter. "You know, out here in the middle of nowhere. Is there a chance she might get bored and move on?"

Anne looked at her a little sadly. "I don't know. I think she's become comfortable here. Life is easy for her and she's got used to being out of the rat race. With her successful husband and the house to live in, I would doubt she needs the money. The other thing is, everyone who is 'in the know' says the Handleys think the world of her – they won't have a bad word said against her." She took a sip of her drink. "Your boss is in a commanding position – and she knows it."

Maggie nodded in agreement. It had only taken her a few weeks to realise that and everything Anne said confirmed it.

"Maggie, this is a great place. You haven't told me much about your past and what brought you here – and I'm not asking you to, but don't let one person spoil what you have."

Maggie took a deep breath. "You're right and I won't."

Dusk crept over them and as the first stars began to appear, so came a further, welcome cooling of the air. Maggie made a move to leave. It was late, but she was reluctant to go. She had enjoyed her time with Anne and for the first time understood the joy that true friendship brings. As she stood by her car, waving goodbye to Tom, Anne came to her and embraced her in a warm hug.

"I'm really glad you came to Langley, Maggie," she said. "I don't think you will ever regret it."

It was a good summer. The weather was generally fine with two or three heatwaves which brought visitors to the park out in numbers. Most of them came to paddle and cool off in the river, but many found their way into the Langley gardens and the new businesses profited beyond expectations.

Maggie never looked back. She was comfortable living at the Petersons' farm, and though she couldn't wait for her own cottage, she was more than happy with Irene and the ever silent Jack. She looked forward to the weekends, exploring the countryside with Rupert as her companion, and she was a regular visitor to Anne and Tom's for Sunday lunch.

As for work, she became ever more efficient in her duties, and gradually learned the best way to handle Geraldine; knowing when to approach her and when to stay out of the way. She enjoyed seeing new stock arrive in the shop; outdoor furniture, garden gifts, plants, and particularly art and decorative interior items. She watched with interest as new ideas were tried and tested and sometimes she caught herself thinking that Geraldine had made a mistake with her choice, though she would never dare to pass comment. More than once in those first months, she watched with silent satisfaction as Geraldine cancelled orders for one product and replaced them with a design Maggie had secretly preferred.

Above all, Maggie felt safe and free at Langley. Apart from a single telephone call to her father to let him know where she was, she had cut herself off from her old life. At first she had been anxious that Adam would track her down. But as the weeks went by she worried less, and for the first time she could remember, she was enjoying life. She found herself looking forward to the next day, and then realising, particularly when Geraldine was absent, that a whole day had passed by without any feelings of unease. Now she didn't clock watch as she had before. She remembered the minutes slipping by on the bank clock, counting down the time for her to go home; the minutes on the kitchen wall clock counting down to Adam's return, day after day, week after week. Time now seemed to race along effortlessly without any sense of impending dread.

Only at night did visions and memories of the past return to haunt her. Occasionally she woke, convinced that Adam was next to her; a horrible aching emptiness inside her. For awful moments she believed it was her new life that was the dream. Then she would hear the cockerel crowing and cows calling across the fields, and she would cry with relief. And so three months had slipped blissfully by, when Maggie arrived at her office as usual. The door between the offices was open and as Maggie listened to Geraldine speaking, she wondered if it had been left ajar on purpose.

"You're making an assumption here, George, that I intend to keep her on." Maggie froze, listening. At least Pam wasn't around to catch her eavesdropping.

George made a comment to which Geraldine replied, "She's all right – she's an office girl; she does what I ask of her and no more than that." Maggie heard the familiar click of the cigarette lighter accompanied by the tinkle of the gold charms. "Well, I'm glad you like her – but she doesn't work for you. Actually, she's like a timid mouse – I find her quite irritating much of the time. Yes, yes – fair enough, I'll tell her to call over and see you."

Maggie heard the telephone being replaced and Geraldine walking quickly towards the door. Maggie scuttled to the cabinet and opened a drawer, busying herself in a file. She was determined not to give Geraldine the pleasure of knowing she'd heard, but try as she might, her burning cheeks threatened to give her away.

"That was George Parkinson," Geraldine said. "Apparently they've got a little place for you. Don't get too excited, it's not much – something small and suitable for someone living alone. Go over and see him."

The 'living alone' comment was not lost on Maggie. *She can't let me have a moment's pleasure*, she thought.

"That's wonderful news, Geraldine, thank you for passing the message to me."

"I'm not just some sort of messenger for George Parkinson," Geraldine snapped. "The reason you have accommodation is because I have authorised it. To be honest I was thinking of letting you go, but I can't face going through the whole recruitment process again. So, you have me to thank for the lucky position in which you find yourself."

"Of course, I understand and thank you very much." Maggie's mouth was dry and her voice sounded hoarse.

The irritation Geraldine had described moments before now reflected in her face and she turned on her heels and disappeared back into her office, swinging the door closed behind her.

Maggie tried not to let Geraldine's put-down spoil the occasion as she drove across the estate to George Parkinson's office. Her stomach fluttered with anticipation as visions of pretty stone cottages with mullioned windows and roses over the door played in her mind.

"It's not much to look at, Maggie, but I think it will do you for a start."

George was sitting behind his desk, the smoke from his large cigar filling the room. He passed a black and white photograph and a door key across the desk. Maggie picked up the photo and studied it. It showed a modern-looking bungalow squashed between two houses on the main street of Bransby village.

"It was built about twenty years ago in the sixties. We could get away with building houses in those days that were not – how should I put it – in keeping with their surroundings," George said, pulling a guilty face.

Maggie tried not to show any disappointment.

"We built four bungalows like that one with retired workers in mind. But this is free at the moment and I know you're eager to get something. I should think you're getting a little tired of life at the Petersons."

"Oh, it's been fine. They have made me feel so welcome and at home – though I'm not sure I know Jack much more now that when I arrived."

George laughed. "Don't be fooled by Jack, he'll be taking it all in and storing it up here." He tapped his forehead with the fingers holding his cigar. "Anyway, what do you think?" He inclined his head towards the photograph in Maggie's hand.

It had never occurred to her that she would turn the offer of a cottage down, whatever it looked like.

"Oh, it will be great. Just to get a place of my own will be wonderful."

This was what Maggie had been waiting for. This was the final step in making a life for herself.

George studied Maggie as she gazed at the photograph.

"How are you finding the job?"

"I'm enjoying it. I think I've got to grips with what's expected of me now and – well, I'm just left to get on with it."

"That's good. What about working for Geraldine?"

Maggie was a little taken aback. She hadn't expected him to ask such a question so directly and she wondered if he had guessed Geraldine's response to the early offer of a cottage. As much as she knew what she wanted to say, she understood what she should say.

"I think she must trust me because she leaves me alone most of the time. Actually, I don't see that much of her."

"No. She's certainly a busy lady." He continued to survey Maggie. He seemed to be trying to read her, and she felt herself blushing.

"Well, I'll go and look at the bungalow, and let you know," she said, wanting to escape his gaze.

"Maggie," George said, as she reached the door, "there is another property coming available, though it might not be right for you – it's in a bit of a lonely spot."

Maggie felt her heart skip a beat and the skin on her arms and neck prickled.

"Not Keeper's Cottage?" she whispered, the blood rushing in her ears.

"As a matter of fact – yes. How did you know?"

Maggie didn't know how, she just knew. She stood still, speechless.

"I'm guessing from your response, it wouldn't be right for you. I have to say, I'm not sure it's the sort of place for a young woman on her own."

"Oh, no." Maggie realised she'd shouted. "I mean yes, Mr Parkinson, absolutely yes. I would love to live there – I truly could not have chosen a better place anywhere." She felt a rush of excitement rapidly followed by concern. Surely a mistake had been made. "Isn't it kept for the trainee agent?" she asked, now fearing she would jog his memory and the offer would be withdrawn.

"That's what it's been used for in recent years. You might not have heard, but Mark is leaving us – finally," he said, "and we've decided not to take on another trainee for a year or two. So the cottage will be free – after next week as it happens. Mark is off to Scotland and the people he's going to are keen to have him right away. Why don't you wait until he's gone, then take a look at the place and see how you feel? I know it's only a mile or so from the manor, but there are no other properties in that side of the park, so it's a bit cut-off. To tell the truth, it's been a little neglected over the past few years – not inside, but the garden will take some managing. I'll keep the bungalow open for you in case you prefer it."

Maggie began to panic as she listened to George talking himself out of the offer.

"Mr Parkinson, I've seen the cottage, I've walked past it and looked down on it from the hillside. I know it's on its own, but I already love it so much. I can't tell you what it would mean to me to be able to live there. And I will look after it – I will never neglect it." Maggie doubted she had ever spoken so passionately about anything.

The corners of George's mouth twitched. "And there was me thinking it would be a hard sell, trying to get someone to live at Keeper's Cottage out of choice." He thought for a second or two. "It is bigger than the bungalow and suitable for a couple or small family, but I don't have anyone else waiting at present – so it's yours if you want it."

Caught somewhere between shock and elation Maggie could only whisper, "I do."

11

The Stranger

MAGGIE HAD RESISTED THE temptation to go to look at Keeper's Cottage. She didn't want to appear to be rushing Mark out. Even so, she found it hard to contain her excitement. She had confided in Anne, who was delighted, and of course the Petersons. Irene and Jack were pleased, but couldn't hide their concern. Like George, they felt it was too lonely a spot for a young woman alone. Maggie reassured them, and even Irene had to accept that her young lodger had no such concerns and was elated.

It was on the last day of August that Maggie stood in a daze before the cottage. She had been drawn to the building the moment she'd seen it on that strange spring morning. Now she hesitated by the front door, barely able to believe that this could be her home.

She opened the front door and despite the coolness of the day she was greeted by unexpected warmth and the comforting smell of woodsmoke.

The cottage was an unusual shape. There was one main living room and that room was impressive. It was octagonal in shape with a high ceiling and the three large sash windows she'd seen from the outside, which looked out across the parkland and to Langley Edge beyond. An old, but serviceable carpet covered the floor and the handsome grey marble fireplace was ruined by an ugly electric fire that had been set into it.

To the rear was a double bedroom. It wasn't large but had two windows, both facing onto the garden at the back, giving it a bright and airy feel. The original fireplace created a striking feature. A third room was designed for use as a second bedroom, but would also make a useful dining room or snug. The kitchen was the most surprising. It was much larger than anyone would guess from the outside and big enough for a table and four chairs. The look was completed by a range of units that appeared to have been fitted recently. The kitchen seemed oversized compared to the rest of the cottage, but it added to the overall feeling of unexpected space.

Maggie looked around for the source of the warmth but could find nothing. The storage heaters were cold and the open fires clearly unused. The cottage felt welcoming, but also something else – a feeling she couldn't define. She was undeniably pleased and yet at the same time, for a reason she couldn't explain, she felt a little unsettled.

Behind the building, a large garden was enclosed by iron railings and beyond that, an area of overgrown ground, separated from the park by railings to three sides. The cottage, the garden and the rough ground sat like an island in the surrounding grassland and marshes. Some people would have found it isolated, even positioned as it was, within the park and not far from the manor, but to Maggie it was paradise.

She took a third look around the inside, now assessing what she would need to purchase just to cover her basic needs. She stood in the bedroom gazing around at the empty space. In her excitement, she had forgotten about the cost of furnishing an empty home. Still, she thought, she wouldn't need much to get started.

The sweet smell of woodsmoke caught her attention again and for a moment she was certain she could feel the warmth from a fire catching the backs of her legs.

"Mary." The voice called so loudly, the man could have been in the room with her.

Maggie jumped, her breath catching in her throat as she spun to face the open door to the hallway, expecting to see a stranger. There was no one and when she turned to the fireplace it was empty and cold.

Maggie ran to the front door and yanked it open. Her heart pounded as she stepped with relief into the open air. She had barely caught her breath before George Parkinson pulled up in his car. She had told him when she would be looking around the cottage and he'd said he would come down if he had a chance. She hadn't expected he would.

"Hello there, Maggie," he called in a jovial voice. "Do you still like it – or have you changed your mind?" His face was serious but the glimmer in his eyes told her he was joking.

Maggie's nerves were jangling. The voice had to be someone outside, in the park, and surely she had just imagined smoke and heat from the fire. She took a deep breath in an effort to calm herself. There was no way she was going to ruin this opportunity.

"There's not a chance I'll change my mind, Mr Parkinson. It's wonderful — and bigger than I thought." Maggie pushed the door open for him to enter.

"Yes, it's surprising when you get inside, isn't it? I see Mark's not left it in too bad a state," he said, looking into each room in turn.

"No, I'll give it a good clean over the weekend and move in as soon as I can. I can't wait."

"Well, it's not often I see people quite so delighted with the cottages on the estate. It's good to see."

"It feels so warm and welcoming. I think Mark must have had an open fire — perhaps in the bedroom. You can still smell the woodsmoke in there."

George sniffed the air. "No, there hasn't been an open fire in this place since the storage heaters were put in back in the seventies. Well, at least I hope not because the chimneys have been capped off." He shook his head. "Not that I'd put it past Mark to have a go."

"Oh, well," Maggie said, "whatever it is, the cottage feels homely."

Together they walked outside and looked at the overgrown garden. The grass on what should be a lawn was knee high and the shrubs and trees around the edge encroached towards the cottage. Some of the bushes inside the six-foot railings had grown so high they were clambering through the bars and over the top, like prisoners trying to escape. Standing alone, to the edge of the would-be lawn stood the yew tree, leaning precariously to the north, its roots clinging on doggedly to keep it from falling. Maggie walked to it, resting her hand on the trunk as though to support it.

"Won't be long before that goes," George said, nodding towards the yew. Then he made a sweeping gesture with his hand. "Looks like you've got your work cut out. How are you going to tackle all this?"

"Please don't worry – I'm looking forward to getting started. I've always wanted a garden. I'll spend this autumn and winter sorting it out – you won't recognise it in the spring."

Maggie distracted George's attention away from the garden. "Can you tell me anything about the place – you know, why it's here all on its own? I think it looks like a gatehouse without the gate."

"You've got it right. It was a gatehouse." George pointed to the grassed track to the side of the cottage where his car now stood behind Maggie's. "That was once another entrance into Langley. The road skirted the marshes to a bridge over the river until – I think it was the 1890s – a flood washed it away. For whatever reason – probably finances – the bridge was never rebuilt and the road fell into disuse."

"I never thought about the river flooding – has it ever reached the cottage?"

"Not that I know of, but when you look on old maps, you can see that the marshland grew significantly after that flood. Keeper's Cottage never used to be this close to the reed beds."

"That's something else I enjoy… seeing and hearing the birds. I'm so passionate about the countryside and wildlife." She looked back at the cottage. "This is my dream home."

"Well, I'm satisfied if you are," George said, walking back to his car. "Move in whenever you're ready."

"Thank you, Mr Parkinson, I can't tell you what it means to me."

"I think I can see what it means to you. I tell you what, I've got some old plans to the place filed away somewhere. I'm sure you'll find them interesting – I'll drop them round to you."

"Thank you." Maggie watched him leaving and then remembered the man's voice. "By the way, just before you arrived, I heard a man calling to someone called Mary. He sounded close by – did you hear him, only I thought I heard the same thing here once before?"

"No, didn't hear or see anyone – you'll probably find that someone who walks in the park has a dog called Mary. You'd be surprised what people call their dogs nowadays."

Maggie watched George drive away, chuckling inwardly at the memory of Jack's disdain for the name Rupert.

Reluctant to leave, Maggie looked around the garden once more, and then followed the track George had pointed out. Where she parked her Escort, the track felt like a solid road and here and there worn cobbles were still visible. But within a few yards, the earth had reclaimed the ground and the cobbles vanished beneath soil and thick grasses. It was just a ten-minute walk to the river. The water flowed swiftly on the far side beneath a steep, stony bank. On the near, more shallow side, the river was captured in gentle eddies, guided into the edges of the marsh. On the opposite bank only the faintest trace of the old road could be seen by those who knew what to look for. Slabs of cut stone lay in the water, remnants of the lost bridge. Maggie could imagine it proudly spanning the river, people on foot standing aside as smart horses and carriages crossed on their journeys to and from the manor. It was sad that it was no longer there, she thought.

Back in the cottage, Maggie hesitated just for a moment before going inside. When she entered, the smell of smoke had gone. She walked from room to room, the air now fresh and cool. The atmosphere had changed completely in a way she couldn't define – not better or worse, just different. She shook her head in puzzlement and then locked the door behind her.

Within a few days, Maggie had spent all of her savings on necessities for the cottage. Anne had been a huge help, giving her a few pieces of worn furniture, including an old sofa, and a drop-leaf table and two chairs. Now all that remained was for her to pack her personal belongings into her car.

As excited as she was at the thought of moving into Keeper's Cottage, Maggie was sad to leave the Petersons' farm. This was where she had found sanctuary following the years of despair with Adam; this was where she had first felt free and safe. Irene, and Jack in his own way, had made her feel welcome and wanted. And as for Rupert – he had become a true friend and companion.

The first week of September brought with it a blast of autumn, with the earliest frost Jack said he could remember for some years. Maggie stood in the kitchen doorway rubbing her hands.

"Well, that's me ready. I'd better get going."

Irene turned from the sink, her face was red and she blew her nose into a large white hanky.

"We're going to miss you, love, aren't we, Jack?" she said, eyes brimming with tears. "Such a quiet little thing you are; isn't she, Jack? But it won't be the same when you've gone."

Jack was sitting at the kitchen table, old newspaper spread out, polishing a pair of battered boots. "Aye," he said.

Maggie swallowed the lump in her own throat and smiled.

"Well, listen, I'm only a few miles up the valley. I can call for a coffee any time and you must come and see the cottage too." Rupert wandered over and pushed a nose into her hand. "I'll come and take this one for a hike as often as possible – if that's all right."

"Oh, of course it is, he'll be lost without you," Irene said, blowing her nose again.

"Take 'im with you," muttered Jack, without looking up from his boot.

"Oh, Jack, that's a smashing idea." Irene beamed. "One less dog around here is fine by me. And he would be such good company for you – you being on your own."

Maggie was shocked. "Do you mean it – I could take Rupert to live with me?"

"Aye, that's what I said." Jack looked up, a twinkle in his eyes and the faintest smile on his weathered face. "It ain't no farm dog, that's for sure."

"Oh, that's right, Jack. He'd think he was in heaven living with Maggie," Irene said breathlessly.

"Well, I'm at work all day," Maggie pondered out loud, "but it would be easy to go home at lunchtime and let him out for a run." She looked down, rubbing the tall dog's ears. "And you would get a good walk every morning and every evening."

"That's sorted then," said Jack. "Get his lead and take some food to tide 'im over." He looked across at the lurcher. "Go on, Dog," he said with a straight face, "get y'self out of me sight."

So four months after she'd seen it from the hillside above, Maggie settled into Keeper's Cottage. Surrounded by cast-off furniture and a cast-off dog, she couldn't have been more content. The cottage immediately felt like home and despite the shortening days and cooling weather, the little building was bright and warm.

On the following Saturday, the one piece of furniture she'd wanted from new, a bed, arrived. The two delivery drivers, who had spent a long time trying to find the cottage, grumpily manhandled it into the bedroom, while Maggie hung the pretty curtains she'd found cheap on the local market. She then put on the matching bed covers and viewed her work with satisfaction. After more uncomfortable nights on the sofa than she cared to remember, she was looking forward to the luxury of a mattress.

The letter box rattled and for the first time she heard Rupert bark. He was never going to be much of a guard dog – he was far too friendly, but nonetheless Maggie was pleased that he was making his presence known. She went to the door, assuming it was the postman, who to her amazement included Keeper's Cottage on his round. Instead, she saw George Parkinson driving away, and a brown envelope lying on the floor.

Inside the envelope she discovered two sets of plans for the cottage. George had dropped them off as he'd promised.

"What a kind man he is," Maggie said to Rupert, who looked up at her, his tail waving.

The two sets of plans told Maggie more about the old gatehouse – including the fact that it wasn't as old as she'd imagined. Many of the cottages in Bransby were 300 or even 400 years old, but the first plan showed that Keeper's Cottage had been built in 1841. However, a note attached to the plan mentioned the demolition of a cottage on the site and the use of some of the stone in the building of the new property.

It appeared from the drawings that there had originally been the one large, octagonal living room, one bedroom to the rear, and a tiny kitchen with a back door also to the rear. At some point the additional room had been added.

According to the second set of plans dated 1952, the old kitchen had been knocked into the adjoining bedroom and a second window added where the closed-off back door had been. Two small, attached stone outhouses had been utilised to make space for a modern bathroom and then a brand new kitchen had been built onto the north side of the cottage. Maggie was fascinated by the changes the building had seen. She ran her fingers over the first plan, picturing how tiny the place had been back then and trying to imagine who might have lived there; people now long forgotten.

Having done as much as she could inside, Maggie spent the remainder of the weekend working in the garden. This was what she enjoyed the most; cutting and sawing at the overgrown shrubbery, not caring about the scratches appearing on her arms and hands. She made a bonfire and sat with a mug of coffee, watching the thick smoke swirl out across the park, and laughing out loud at Rupert as he tried unsuccessfully to catch the voles and mice disturbed from the undergrowth.

"Morning – looks like you've got some hard work to do."

Maggie jumped up, startled, coffee slopping over the edges of the mug. The man stood a little way back from the garden rails and then advanced nonchalantly towards the gate, a confident, relaxed smile on his face. As he approached he brought his fingers to his lips and let out an ear-splitting whistle. This brought, from somewhere in the direction of the reed beds, a short, rough-coated terrier scurrying back to him, tail wagging furiously.

The man seemed to realise that he had startled Maggie and his smile broadened still further as he reached the garden gate.

"I'm so sorry if I made you jump. I've seen you walking a few times in the park with your dog. I didn't know you lived here." He reached down and patted his terrier who was sniffing noses with a very happy Rupert on the other side of the gate. "I've met the chap who lives here," he continued, "but I didn't realise you lived here, too."

Maggie found herself staring at the man as he spoke. He was leaning his stocky frame against the gate in a completely relaxed fashion, as though passing the time of day with an old friend. She watched his unruly brown hair ruffling in the breeze and the light shining in his dark eyes.

She became aware of her own scruffy appearance; her tied-back hair fallen in strands around her face, her arms covered in dirt and blood from the scratches. A hot flush of embarrassment rushed across her face as she tried to capture the escaped tresses and push them behind her ear. The man, aware of her discomfort, extended a hand through the gate.

"Sorry, I should've introduced myself." His smile expanded. "Philip Sheldon – it's nice to meet you. At last I get the chance to speak to you and start off by scaring you half to death." He laughed at his joke.

She took his hand. "Maggie Armstrong," she said, feeling the need to explain while her face continued to burn. "The man you met – Mark, doesn't live here anymore; he's moved away with a new job. I work for Langley and I've just moved in." For a second she thought of adding *alone*, but didn't.

"Wow, what a great place to live. And Bracken has certainly found a new pal. How about letting yours out so they can meet properly? What's his name?"

Maggie opened the gate. "This is Rupert."

"Great name," Philip said with a straight face.

"I didn't come up with it, but I couldn't imagine him being called anything else now."

The dogs made a fuss of each other; the tall lurcher standing over the short-legged Bracken. They sniffed nose to nose, then the terrier went down on her forelegs and took off, tail tucked under in mock fright, a delighted Rupert in hot pursuit.

The young man laughed out loud as he watched the dogs disappearing across the park.

"That's one way of tiring them out," he said.

"That's true," Maggie said, finding herself watching the man rather than the dogs.

When the dogs returned, breathless with tongues lolling, Philip knelt down on one knee to bring him eye level with Rupert.

"You're a handsome chap, aren't you?" he said, rubbing the dog's ears. "To tell you the truth it was the dog I recognised first when I spotted him in the garden."

Maggie couldn't say she'd ever noticed Philip before. She tried to think of something to say.

"Well, perhaps we'll see each other again." She looked down as she spoke.

"I hope so."

Maggie continued to avoid eye contact.

"Well, I'll tell you what, Maggie; if these two spot each other, there's no way we'll avoid meeting." He called his dog. "Come on, Bracken. We'll leave you in peace. It was great to meet you."

He strode away, the dog at his heels. "It was nice to meet you, too," Maggie whispered and doubted he heard her.

That night, Maggie drifted off to sleep to the memory of wavy brown hair, dark, kind eyes and a smiling face.

Early next morning, she was shaken from her sleep by the sound of thunder and hail battering against the window. The autumn storms had been forecast and arrived with dramatic effect.

When the worst of the lightning had passed, Maggie set off for her usual morning walk with Rupert. She was an early riser, seldom staying in bed after six, and the hour's walk she took each morning wasn't a chore.

She followed the path by the marshes and then climbed up to the highest part of the park below Langley Wood. Continuing in a wide arc, she worked her way back towards Keeper's Cottage and as she walked, a low drawn-out rumble announced the arrival of another storm.

Heron Brook ran down from Langley Wood, across the park and into the marshes. A culvert took it beneath the road from the manor, but further up the park, a small footbridge was provided for walkers. The brook had been dry for most of the summer, and this was the first time Maggie had needed to use the rickety crossing. Now, following the storm, a torrent of water rushed down just inches beneath the wooden planks. She crossed the bridge and turned towards Keeper's Cottage, bending into the gusting wind that ran ahead of the storm. Hailstones stung her face and bounced along the ground, and Rupert huddled behind her, ears flat and his tail tucked beneath him.

As she approached the cottage, lightning streaked across the sky, the thunder clap following only a second or two later. She quickened her pace and glanced up into the wind, holding her hat on with one hand. From nowhere came a sudden rush of fear. She had never been scared of storms, but now she shuddered in panic. Even though the cottage was in sight, Maggie was overwhelmed by the feeling that she had gone too far from home and must get back. As she broke into a run she glanced up into the driving hail and rain. A man was walking towards her. He was on the path, fifty yards ahead and close to the cottage. She felt a surge of relief. She was so pleased to see him; to know she wasn't alone. As she hurried towards him, she noted that he wore some sort of short jacket and no hat. A medium-sized brown dog trotted at his left side and he strolled at a leisurely pace towards her, seemingly unperturbed by the weather. He was close enough for her to make out his straggly grey hair and perhaps the shadow of stubble on his face. He raised his hand as though in acknowledgement and she found herself waving back, feeling an unexpected surge of joy.

Lightning forked to the ground not far away followed instantly by the deafening crash of thunder. Maggie glanced down to check that Rupert was close by, and then looked up. She stopped dead. The path before her was completely deserted. There was no sign of the man or his dog.

12

A Chance Meeting

"I DON'T BELIEVE IN ghosts," Maggie said.

She was sitting with Anne in a corner of the Stag Inn. The oppressive atmosphere in the old building seemed to add eeriness to her tale.

"Well, you give me another explanation." Anne's eyes twinkled with intrigue.

"It had to be just an ordinary man walking in the park and he darted for cover from the storm." Even as she spoke the words, Maggie knew that wasn't possible. "And where exactly did he dart to – in all of three seconds?"

"I don't know, but he must have done that. Although there was something peculiar about him…" Maggie's voice trailed off as her mind drifted back, trying to capture the detail of what she'd seen. "I'm just not sure what… and for a moment I thought I recognised him."

"Who did you think he was?"

Maggie closed her eyes, trying to picture the man. "It's like when you're trying to remember a name or a place and it's on the tip of your tongue but won't come." She shook her head in exasperation. "Perhaps he looked like someone I've seen at Langley – that's all I can think of."

"Well, when you see him again – take a closer look. We need details," Anne said, finishing off her drink. "What about Rupert? How did he behave?"

"He seemed nervous – which isn't like him at all. Perhaps it was just the thunder. When we got to the cottage he was fine."

"They say dogs can pick these things up. Doesn't sound like it was the storm to me."

"Anne, will you stop it?" Maggie said, scolding her friend's mischievous determination to scare her. "Anyway, are you saying you believe there are such things as ghosts? I mean, have you ever seen one?"

"Yes and no. Yes, I believe that there are things we don't fully understand. Too many sensible people have had experiences that can't be explained. And regrettably no, I've never seen one. But I'd love to."

Maggie got up to go. "Well, I wouldn't," she said, "and I hope I don't see him again – ghost or not."

As they left, Maggie followed her friend through the bar and past the roaring log fire where a small group of staff members from the garden centre were gathered around a table. They were laughing and joking over their drinks, the light from the flames dancing behind them. Maggie waved to two of the people she recognised and felt a glow of satisfaction when they waved back. As she squeezed past a few people waiting at the bar, static tingling ran up her arms and down her neck. She shuddered.

The man was standing behind the group, resting an arm on the mantelpiece of the fire and holding a pipe to his mouth. He was looking directly at Maggie. His grey hair hung in strands almost to his shoulders and dark stubble covered his haggard face. He was utterly motionless, and appeared out of focus, separated from the others by swirls of smoke. The laughter in the room faded and became muffled. As Maggie stared into his drawn face, the faintest glimmer of a sad smile appeared on his thin lips, and for a fleeting moment she wanted to go to him. She tore her eyes away to where Anne had walked on ahead and called her friend back. When she turned to point to the man he was no longer there.

"Are you okay? You've gone terribly pale."

"I'm fine," Maggie whispered. She wanted to tell Anne what she'd seen, but she couldn't. It all seemed so unreal. She had seen the man twice in the same day and on each occasion he had vanished. For a horrible moment she feared she was losing her mind as the ancient walls of the inn seemed to close in on her. A surge of nausea came over her and she scrambled past Anne, desperate to get out of the claustrophobic room.

Anne hurried after her. "You don't look fine. Are you sure you're all right?"

"Yes, Anne – thanks. I just felt a bit odd for a minute, that's all," she said, leaning against the outer wall and gulping in deep breaths.

"It does get a bit airless in there," Anne said.

Maggie tried to calm herself, but the image of the man remained vivid in her mind and seeing him again brought back what she'd witnessed that morning with stark clarity.

Anne put a hand on Maggie's shoulder. "You're getting your colour back." She sounded relieved.

"I am feeling better, thanks. And I don't know why, but it's just come to me what was so strange about the man this morning."

"Brilliant," Anne said, ushering Maggie towards their cars. "Come on, what was it?"

"Well, me and Rupert were absolutely drenched – soaked through."

Anne nodded. "As you would expect – out in the middle of a thunderstorm."

"Well, I could see the man's hair wafting as if in a breeze, and his jacket and trousers – the dog's coat, too – they were completely dry."

Maggie settled onto the worn sofa with Rupert curled up beside her. She went over and over the two strange experiences in her head. What had she seen? Had she actually seen anything, or had she imagined it? She thought back to the voices by the oak tree and she worried again that she was suffering some kind of mental trauma. She could picture herself shouting to Anne at the inn, 'Look – there he is, standing by the fire.' And Anne would have rushed to look and only seen the familiar faces of the workers from the manor. The last thing Maggie wanted was for Anne to discover that her new friend was some sort of hallucinating nutcase.

"If it happens again, I will see a doctor, I promise," Maggie said to Rupert. His tail thumped in rhythmic response.

When she went to bed, Maggie read a soppy novel; trying hard to keep the image of the strange man from her mind. It was gone one o'clock before she could bring herself to turn out the light.

When Maggie arrived at work early the next morning, she was surprised to find Pam already there, rattling away on the typewriter with impressive speed. She had taken the last two weeks off and was now clearly on a mission to catch up. Maggie had offered to cover some of her work for her, but Pam had politely declined.

"Morning, Pam, did you have a good few days?" Maggie asked.

"Not especially, but I got a bit of decorating done."

With that, the typewriter sprang into action again and the conversation was over.

Maggie had become used to Pam's reluctance to converse, and as she sorted out the post, she smiled at the irony. For how many years had she been the one who kept to herself and wouldn't talk to anyone? Now that she was starting to enjoy conversations, she found herself ensconced in a small office with someone who seldom spoke more than a few sentences in a day.

She picked up a newly delivered interior magazine and gazed longingly at the photographs. She was studying an oak dresser and a sofa and chairs that would look perfect in Keeper's Cottage, when Geraldine walked in. As usual, she was looking immaculate and wearing a suit Maggie hadn't seen before. It looked expensive.

"Have you got some proper work to do, or do you already fancy yourself as a buyer?" Geraldine said.

Maggie quickly placed the catalogue onto a pile of papers stacked ready to take through to Geraldine's office.

"No. I was just having a quick look."

"Well, look at what you're paid to look at. And get me a coffee."

"Good morning, Geraldine," Pam said chirpily. "I hope you are well."

At first, Maggie thought Pam was trying to rescue her by deflecting Geraldine's attention.

"Morning, Pam, I'm fine thanks. It's good to have you back. Have you had an enjoyable break?"

"I did thank you, the weather was beautiful and we got out and about. I'll get your coffee; it's all ready for you – just needs the hot water."

Maggie sat back at her desk, her heart sinking. Her life outside of work could not be better, but here, in the presence of Geraldine, she could feel herself shrinking into a pathetic, weak thing. She felt angry – not at Geraldine or Pam, but with herself.

Geraldine disappeared into her office and returned almost immediately.

"Maggie, I need some sales figures. And I need them quickly." She passed over a list of supplier names. "Christina is coming along in an hour to discuss products for next year and I need the information for then."

Maggie took the list, panicking inside. Most of the information was held in manual ledgers and wasn't easy to find. She grabbed files from the shelves and began her frantic search, all the time hoping Christina Handley would be late.

In the few months Maggie had worked at Langley, she had only met Christina perhaps a dozen times. On each occasion it had been to do little more than deliver cups of coffee or files to Geraldine's office. Christina was a quiet, well-spoken woman in her mid-thirties. She was pretty, wore little make-up, and although she was always well dressed, her clothing looked comfortable and suited to country living. Her long, blonde hair was usually tied back in a ponytail, and she was often accompanied by her black Labrador, Eddie.

All too quickly came the gentle knock at the office door, and Pam rushed to guide Christina Handley towards Geraldine's office.

"Can I get you a drink, Mrs Handley?"

"Yes please, Pam."

"Did you and Mr Handley have a good sailing holiday?" Pam asked.

"Oh, we had the most wonderful time, Pam. Thank you for asking."

She disappeared into Geraldine's office without seeming to notice Maggie.

Maggie continued flicking through files, wondering how on earth Pam knew the Handleys had been sailing, and why she had never mentioned it in conversation.

When Pam returned to her desk, she looked across at Maggie.

"Better crack on with those figures, Maggie, they're waiting."

Why don't you help me, then? Maggie thought, and for the first time began to grasp Pam's true nature. Maggie felt certain it was born out of self-preservation, but nevertheless she found her colleague's behaviour hurtful. She knew at that moment she would never trust Pam.

Maggie entered the adjoining office a few minutes later and stood by the door. Geraldine was reclining in her chair, cigarette already lit. Christine Handley sat on the opposite side of the desk, leafing through a garden furniture catalogue.

"You can see why I think we should go for those, don't you?" Geraldine pointed towards the catalogue, a cigarette between her fingers, the bracelet hanging heavily from her thin wrist.

"I do like them, Geraldine, I just wondered if we should try something a little different next year."

"Well, Christina, you can go for something different, or you can go for something that sells." Geraldine sat back and blew out a cloud of smoke. "Obviously, it's up to you."

Maggie stood still, wondering if they knew she was there. *How can she be so rude?* she thought, silently urging Christina to argue, though already sensing that wouldn't happen.

"No, Geraldine, I'm sure you're right. I'll leave it to you," Christina said with the faintest hint of a sigh.

Geraldine looked up and beckoned Maggie over.

"Come on, Maggie, we haven't got all day." She reached for the file. "Now, Christina, we need to thin out the number of suppliers. Let's look at the sales for this summer and decide who to drop." She looked up to see Maggie still hovering.

"That'll be all, Maggie – and try not to take so long next time."

Maggie hurried away, aware that Christina Handley hadn't looked up once.

That evening, Maggie took Rupert for a stroll before it got dark. The autumn evenings were drawing in and she wanted to take every advantage of the remaining light.

She was still giving herself a firm talking to for allowing Geraldine to upset her. She had felt uncomfortable all day, and realising now that Pam was basking in her discomfort only made matters worse. But as she walked, she felt the magic of the place lift her spirits. She listened to the last evening calls of the birds. The reeds were quieter now that the summer warblers had left for their winter home, but the ducks and moorhens still called from deep within their hiding place.

Suddenly, Rupert raced off, his tail waving in the air. Maggie was wondering who or what he was chasing, when a bedraggled terrier appeared from the marsh and scampered off with the lurcher. A familiar shrill whistle sounded and Philip appeared around a bend on the edge of the reed bed.

"Well, fancy meeting you here," he said. "I was just saying to Bracken, 'I wonder if we'll see Rupert and that girl with the strange name'." There was the mischievous grin and Maggie felt her heart skip. "Do you mind if we walk with you for a while?" he asked.

"No, not at all," Maggie said, looking away towards the playing dogs and praying for the pink in her cheeks to subside.

"I finished work a bit earlier today and thought I'd come over for a stroll. Like I said before, this is a regular haunt for me – I live at Ashburn and like to get out of the town. But what about you? You're lucky enough to live here."

"I am lucky, I know. Now I'm here, I can't imagine being anywhere else."

They walked together for an hour until it was dark, taking a circular route that finished back at the cottage. Maggie found herself becoming unexpectedly relaxed in Philip's company, telling him all about her move to Langley, her job and life with the Petersons before moving to Keeper's Cottage. As usual she skirted around any link to her past. She found her pace slowing as she tried to delay their arrival back at her garden gate.

"I'm sorry you've got to walk back to the manor in the dark," she said. "I could give you a lift in the car."

"Oh, don't worry about that. I don't mind the dark. Anyway, I'll probably run – I have to try and keep fit. It'll only take ten minutes." He looked at her hopefully. "Or, maybe we could go for a quick drink at the inn?"

Maggie had vowed she would steer clear of men. She was certain she could never trust a man again and even if she did – what would they see in her, especially once they got to know her. She felt the deep ache inside her. She had so little to give.

"No. Thank you for asking me but no – not at the moment." She didn't look at him as she spoke.

"Sorry," Philip said, his calm eyes on her. "I never thought – you are probably already with someone. It's only that I just assumed you were on your own."

"No, I'm not with anyone at the moment," she said, trying to sound indifferent. "I just enjoy my own company." She regretted she'd said that.

"Oh, I'm truly sorry, Maggie, for intruding on you like this. It has been lovely talking with you; perhaps I'll see you around here again sometime." He stepped back from the gate but was still facing her, disappointment stealing the shine from his eyes.

The evening had fallen still without even the call of a bird or waft of breeze to ease the silence between them. Philip waited for a long moment and then turned away, calling Bracken to him. Maggie watched him go, desperate to say something, but the confusion in her mind rendering her mute. And then she was calling after him.

"What about next Sunday?"

Phillip stopped and looked back. "What about next Sunday?" he asked with a serious expression but the corners of his mouth twitched upwards.

"I thought it might be nice to walk again – perhaps for a bit further," Maggie said, her voice fading with the dread that he'd changed his mind.

"I'll meet you here at ten for a morning walk – even if it's raining. I'm not one of those fair-weather walkers, you know."

Maggie grinned. "It's a deal."

13

Memories Shared

MAGGIE HAD NEVER BEEN a slave to distraction. Whatever was happening in her life, even the most awful of events, she was able to hide, even disguise, her feelings from the outside world. Now she felt giddy. Every time she thought of the forthcoming Sunday, her heart skipped with a flutter of excitement. She refused to think of it as a date, but even so she felt exhilarated at the thought of meeting Philip again. She was convinced that Pam and even Geraldine would see a mysterious change in her, but if they did, they made no comment.

It was the September half-year count and the point at which the success of the department so far this season could be measured. This was a new experience for Maggie. Everyone who worked for Geraldine was on hand – even those who usually worked in the restaurant and normally had little to do with the shop. Maggie had a great time, clambering about into the far corners and onto the high dusty shelves of the stockroom, making sure every item was accounted for. She finished her first designated area then moved to the garden centre where she listed some of the larger items including outside chairs and tables.

The process brought a welcome change to her duties. She was out of the office, mixing with other staff and getting to see the products up close. The only downside was that Geraldine would be around for the entire week. It was an important time for her and the tension she generated as she moved from area to area overseeing the proceedings, suggested she would accept nothing less than the stock count translating into excellent results.

As the evening wore on and the end of the count was in sight, Maggie found her concentration drifting again. Her mind returned to Philip and she began to plan in her head where they might go on Sunday. She noted down the final wooden chairs and benches onto her sheet, and then sat on one of them to rest her aching legs. She gazed up above the old clock tower of the stables towards the wood beyond, now lost in darkness. Perhaps they would walk up there; perhaps they might even go to the oak, she thought. The moon appeared from behind dark clouds, catching the white face of the clock, which sparkled like silver. *Only six days to go,* she thought. Time at Langley had never dragged... until now.

"I hope you've been watching what you're doing and not daydreaming all evening."

Geraldine stood behind Maggie. Pam was standing with her.

"No, I've actually finished," Maggie said, getting to her feet.

Pam smiled as though she knew something Maggie didn't.

"So you think the stocktake is over for you, do you?" Geraldine said with a smirk.

Pam stepped forward to reinforce Geraldine's point.

"You'll be sick of the sight of these sheets by the end of the week, Maggie. You've got all the costings to do. Of course I would have helped you but I'm not in for the rest of the week."

"Don't worry about that, Pam, it will keep her busy for a while," Geraldine said as she walked away.

The next day Maggie started the mundane task described by Pam; finding cost prices and manually calculating the stock value of each sheet. Never had the need for bringing in computerised systems been more apparent to her. She was trying her best to decipher the writing on one of the papers, when Geraldine came in, slamming the door behind her. She marched up to the desk and threw two stock sheets down in front of Maggie.

"There are mistakes on these. I've corrected them."

Maggie picked up the sheet and looked over the alterations. Four pieces of garden furniture had been miscounted and corrected by Geraldine. Maggie felt her heart sink. The altered items were among the things she had recorded herself. She spoke before thinking.

"Are you sure these are wrong, Geraldine? I counted them myself."

Geraldine's face was stony.

"Thank you for bringing your own incompetence to my attention," she snapped. "I suggest you concentrate on your own faults before questioning me."

"I'm sorry," Maggie whispered. "I'll make sure I'm more careful in future."

"I should hope so, too. I will not put up with this kind of shoddy work. The value of that stock would have a real impact on our figures. It's a good job that I do spot checks myself. I wouldn't worry about being more careful in the future, if I was you – I would worry about there being a future." Geraldine turned and stormed into her office.

For the first time at Langley, Maggie found herself fighting back tears. She felt useless. She couldn't believe she had made such stupid mistakes. At lunchtime, she slipped down to the garden centre and checked on the four items she'd got wrong. Geraldine was right, she had miscounted them. There was one item less for each of the lines and apparently there had been no sales during the day. She checked the stockroom to make sure no one had moved them, but they were not to be found. She had clearly counted the same items twice. She knew she'd been daydreaming and she berated herself for the remainder of the day.

The event put a dampener on the rest of the week. With Geraldine in a fouler mood than usual, Maggie did her best to keep out of her way. It was a massive relief when the weekend finally arrived.

A cool autumn breeze blew white clouds quickly across the sky, casting shadows that chased along the ground ahead of Maggie and Philip. The cold night had produced heavy dew and the drenched grass soon soaked the bottoms of their jeans. They chatted and laughed as they walked and it occurred to Maggie that she had never known what it was like to feel safe and relaxed in the company of a man. She realised that she had always been nervous of Adam – even in the early days; as though deep down, an instinctive part of her recognised the hidden danger.

"I can't believe you're a writer," Maggie said, as they headed uphill towards the wood. "That's so glamorous."

"I wouldn't say being a sports writer for a local paper was glamorous, but it's the only job I ever wanted and I was lucky to get it. It took a few years before they let me loose with any actual writing, but now I do a regular column."

"You must let me see what you've written sometime. What sports do you write about?"

"Anything and everything – whatever big is happening at the time. My real love is rugby, but I enjoy most sport."

"It must be wonderful being able to spend every day doing something you enjoy."

"It is. Sometimes it's a bit pressured – you know, deadlines and the like. But I never take for granted what I've got. Anyway, you enjoy working here, don't you?"

"I do love it here – I feel as though I belong, although I'm not sure my boss thinks that."

"Bit of a dragon is he?"

"He's a she and she'd have most dragons for breakfast."

"Blimey, tell me more."

Maggie forced a hollow laugh, but it was only to mask the sinking feeling she had. It felt as though if she even mentioned Geraldine's name, it would somehow sully the perfect day.

"I'll tell you about her another time," she said. "Look — this is where you get a great view of Keeper's Cottage."

They had reached Heron Brook by the footbridge. The raging torrent from the morning of the storm had returned to a gentle trickle of crystal-clear water. Rupert and Bracken jumped into the stream for a drink, frightening off a moorhen, which cackled in alarm. They crossed the bridge and then turned to look back the way they'd come.

"Who wouldn't want to make their life in a place like this if they got the chance?" Philip said.

"That's what I thought when I first saw it. I still can't believe I'm here. Sometimes I'm certain I will wake up and find myself back in the city." Maggie fell silent, taking in the view she was coming to know so well, her eyes following the contours of the downs on the skyline to the chalk path she had followed that first day to the woods and the river. She hadn't been certain until that moment that she would take Philip to the oak tree.

"Can I show you somewhere that is very special to me? Somewhere I haven't shown anyone else."

"Sounds too intriguing to say no."

Maggie led the way as they began the steep zig-zag climb up the hillside, the dogs racing off ahead, on the scent of hares. A half-hour later and they reached the oak tree. Maggie placed her hand on the trunk, her fingers tracing over the rough bark. She hesitated – waiting. Like before, nothing happened, though she still sensed the peace and tranquillity that emanated from the place.

She led Philip to the rocky edge and they sat on the flat stone together looking down on the park; the cottage tiny in the distance. The first hint of autumn colour touched the trees and the rowans on the steep bank below hung heavy with red berries. Spiders' webs clung to the bracken and shrubs, draped in droplets of dew that glittered jewel-like in the sunshine.

"What a great place. I've never been up here before – it really is stunning," Philip said.

"It's more than that – I don't know what it is but it feels special. You know – special to me. I know this sounds silly, but I feel safe here – as though the trees and the rocks and the earth know me and will look after me." She blushed, embarrassed. She couldn't – wouldn't – tell him more than that.

Philip seemed to sense her discomfort. "I don't think it's silly. I think I know what you mean," he said. "On the farm where we lived when I was growing up – I had a favourite place. It was by a pond in our meadow. The first really horrible thing I can recall was when my grandfather died. I would be about six, but I can remember it so well. All the adults being upset; actually seeing my father cry for the first time." He smiled wryly. "The only time, come to think of it."

Maggie watched him as he spoke; his dark eyes were soft, his thick eyebrows unruly like his wavy hair, and his hands, resting on the rock as he leaned back, were strong and brown. She felt the butterflies in her stomach. It was as though the same magnetic draw that had led her to this place was now pulling her to him.

"Anyway," Philip continued, seemingly unaware of the effect he had upon her, "the only place I wanted to be was down by the pond – like this place is for you, I felt safe there. I sat for ages, you know, just trying to understand it all. That was until I was missed – then all hell let loose; scared the lot of them to death when they couldn't find me." He looked at Maggie. "It's strange the things you remember and the things you forget, isn't it?"

Maggie nodded. "Some things you want to forget." She looked into his kind face. "And some things you want to remember – like now." She looked away.

He turned to her, unable to hide the surprise on his face. He reached over and squeezed her hand gently. "I've enjoyed today, too."

He took his hand away and Maggie felt a pang of disappointment. Plucking with her nails at an emerald cushion of moss on the rock, she tried to think of something to say. Rupert came to the rescue, lying panting by her side while Bracken scurried about tirelessly in the undergrowth. As she ruffled his fur and stroked his ears, his presence eased her nerves.

"Tell me some more about yourself – do you have a family – brothers or sisters?" she said.

"Well, my father is a farmer. I've got two older brothers and a younger sister. I love the farm, but I never wanted to be a farmer. Lucky for me, I've never been put under any pressure. My oldest brother, Rob, is keen to take up the family tradition." Philip grinned. "Dad still wasn't impressed when I started writing, though."

"I'm so envious of you, being part of a big family. You know, people around who care about you – and growing up on a farm, too. You must have wonderful childhood memories."

"Well, we always got on okay. My big brothers did look after me I suppose, though it didn't stop me getting into a few scrapes." He stretched over to a small stick that lay within arm's reach and threw it for Bracken down the slope. She scuttled after it, oblivious to the steep terrain and found it quickly amongst the rocks. "Anyway, what about you, what sort of childhood did you have? Let's have one of your memories."

"I don't know. I don't seem to have any strong memories, other than when my mother died. I was a bit older than you when you lost your grandfather – nine, actually."

"God, Maggs, I'm so sorry."

No one had ever called her Maggs. She liked it.

"No – it's okay. I'm glad I was old enough to remember her. She was kind, a good mum." Maggie captured the image of her mother in her mind and held it there, like studying a photograph. "I think now, looking back, that she was also quite sad."

"What makes you think that? Do you know why?"

Maggie silently shook her head, even though she knew the answer. She changed the subject.

"Actually, when you mentioned about a pond on your farm, it reminded me of something I'd completely forgotten about until quite recently. I was really young and I can't remember exactly where we were – we moved around quite a bit with my dad's job. It's a very disjointed memory, just snippets and images... but we buried some kind of box or jar in the garden by our pond. It was a heavy thing with leaves carved around it." She smiled at the memory. "I can see my little hands trying to hold it – it was really hefty. We each put a favourite thing in it then Dad put a big stone on top and buried it. Then we planted a bush on top."

"Sounds like a time capsule to me. I can remember doing one at school."

"Yes, we did, too, but this was at home. Dad was there and I don't know, perhaps one of his friends. I can't remember Mum being there but she must have been because I would have only been about four or five."

"Crikey, you've got a good memory."

"I think it must have meant something to me at the time."

"Can you remember what you put in the box?"

"Do you know, I can. And the strange thing is that recently I've dreamt about it. It was a small toy horse, carved out of wood. It must have been special to me at the time. Perhaps something has reminded me of it and it has come back to me in dreams."

"Maybe you had the toy at a time when you were very happy – and now you are happy again," Philip said, taking up her hand once more.

Maggie looked from Philip to the cottage and back again. "Perhaps that's what it is."

They walked back, sharing more about themselves as they strolled.

"You'll have to come and watch me play rugby some time, I play most Saturdays," Philip said, as they arrived at the cottage.

Maggie observed his average frame – two or three inches below six feet she guessed.

"You don't look like a rugby player."

"I might not be big – but I'm mighty fast; and better looking than the big guys."

He looked directly at her, smiling and waiting for Maggie to agree. She kept a straight face and with her head tilted she pursed her lips as though having to give the comment serious consideration.

"I'll come to see you play," Maggie said. "Then I can compare you to the rest of the team."

Philip opened the car to let a tired Bracken jump into the back and Maggie watched him whilst agonising about asking him in for a coffee. He made it easy for her.

"I've really enjoyed the walk," he said. Then he reached out and took her hand in his. "But I've enjoyed your company more." He looked at her unwaveringly. "Can I take you out for a meal one evening this week?"

Maggie's stomach did a somersault. Could it really be that he actually liked her?

"Yes, Philip," she said quietly. "I would like that."

Before she could react, he leaned forward and kissed her gently on the cheek, then reached down to Rupert, who was standing between them, and gave him a scratch along his back.

"I'll give you a call and let you know when." He got into his car and wound down the window. "By the way, it's Phil."

Maggie grinned. "By the way, it's Maggs."

That night, Maggie dreamed that someone was alongside her in bed. Strong arms were enveloping her, pulling her towards him. This time she didn't struggle or cry out, as she snuggled up against the warmth of his body. Then she dreamed she had awoken and the birds were singing, chickens clucked outside, and sheep and cattle called in the distance. Woodsmoke filled the air, but somehow she knew she was still in a dream, that she was not yet awake.

The light from the window penetrated Maggie's eyelids, but she refused to open them. She lay still; warm and cosy in bed, remembering yesterday and smiling. Then she heard a distinct sound from within the bedroom; a comforting and familiar noise. It was the sound of metal on metal as a poker raked cold ashes back and forth through the grate of the fire. She'd heard it so many times before – it was a sound of warmth, comfort and safety.

"Mary." The man's voice whispered close to her ear, his breath caressing her cheek.

Maggie sat bolt upright staring wildly around the room. All was silent and still. The fireplace, partly obscured by a large bowl and jug standing on the hearth, stood cold and unused.

14

A Threat

THE EERINESS OF THE experience was hard for Maggie to shake off. She tried to be logical. Surely it had been a dream. She'd heard a man calling the name Mary on more than one occasion and that had played out in a strange half-dream. The idea seemed rational and had the effect of calming her nerves, though for several nights she struggled to get to sleep and woke often, unconsciously listening.

Now, two weeks later, Maggie stood by the leaning yew tree in the garden surveying the results of her hard work. The shrubs and bushes were cut back; buddleias and fuchsias carefully trimmed to ensure an abundance of flowers in the summer, and the crop of stubborn groundsel and dandelions removed from the borders. She had mowed the lawn for the final time and it would have looked smart but for the scattering of autumn leaves that drifted with the wind and collected in random patterns across the grass. She had raked them up so many times that she pledged not to do it again until the nearby trees had shed the last of their foliage.

A car approached along the road from the manor, and as it came to a halt Maggie was surprised to see George Parkinson.

"Morning, Maggie, I hope you don't mind me calling unannounced. I'm doing a few property checks and thought there might be a chance you were in."

"Of course," Maggie said, trying to remember the state of the cottage inside. "Please, come in and look around."

He smiled. "Don't worry; I would definitely make an appointment for that. I just need to have a quick look at the outside. The place is due for external decorating next year. I just wanted to see how urgent it is. We budget for renovations to a percentage of properties each year, but there are always unexpected problems that mean some jump the queue; leaking roofs and the like." He hesitated for a moment, looking over the garden. "You weren't joking when you said you could handle this, were you? I'm impressed by what you've done."

"Thank you," Maggie said glowing at the compliment. "I've enjoyed every minute – scratches and all."

It took George less than ten minutes to check the outside of the cottage before he headed back to his car. As Maggie watched him leave it occurred to her that she had been inhospitable.

"Would you like a coffee before you go, Mr Parkinson?" she asked, half hoping he would decline.

He turned back with a smile. "I'm not in a hurry so I'll take you up on that. Thank you."

She showed him into the living room and then scurried off in search of her best – or least chipped – cups and saucers. She'd bought them for a few pence off the market and now wished she had spent a little more. A few minutes later she set a tray down between them and sat uneasily opposite him. He had been nothing but kind and encouraging, but still she felt awkward at having someone she thought of as important in the house.

"By the way, Maggie, please call me George."

"Oh, yes, right, Mr... I mean, George." Maggie cringed inside.

She listened with interest as he talked; watching his round face becoming animated with pride as he spoke of his time at Langley. He had worked there for most of his life and he had a great depth of knowledge of the land and the buildings. He told her about the conservation work on the manor and other properties that took place every year, and the constant battle to raise enough funds to keep going.

"What people don't realise is that it is often not straightforward maintenance work we need. We bring in specialists in stone, brick and timber from all around the country – costs a small fortune. So many country estates end up selling their outlying properties off, but we don't want to do that – not if we can help it."

"I have to admit, I'm one of the people who wouldn't think about the cost – it all looks so well looked after," Maggie said.

"That's why Richard has expanded the garden centre and restaurant – we need that extra income. And we are

139

going to need even more if we are ever to embark on the restoration of the south wing." He looked at Maggie intently. "You're playing an important role here towards the future of Langley – always remember that."

Maggie felt a glow inside. Just as he'd done at the interview, George had a way of putting Maggie at her ease and she was proud that he thought the small part she was playing at Langley was important. Soon she found herself speaking of the affection she had already developed for the place. She chatted about exploring the parkland and what she saw; the roe deer and badgers emerging from the wood in the evening; the variety of birds that came into the garden; of listening to tawny owls outside the window, and of her amazement at seeing the stars so clearly at night.

"The reed beds are interesting too, aren't they?" George said. "People don't realise just what lives in them – and depends on them."

"No, I never did. Not until this summer, but the place has been alive with all kinds of birds and frogs, too. I love being so close – when it's still and calm I can hear them from the cottage."

As she talked, a memory came back to Maggie. "I once heard the strangest sound. I'm sure it came from the marshes. It was on the first day I ever came here in the spring and it's hard to describe – like a kind of blowing sound. It reminded me of when I was small and would blow over the top of a milk bottle, but it was louder and deeper – so odd." She didn't mention the even odder events of that day.

George Parkinson raised an eyebrow. "Sounds like you're describing the call of the bittern, though I doubt it could have been." His tone carried more than a note of disbelief.

"A what?" Maggie had never heard the name.

"It's a kind of heron – one of our rarest birds and difficult to see. They're not far off extinct in this country, and I think the last time they were recorded here was perhaps fifty or sixty years ago. You often only know they are there at all when the males call in the spring." George got up to leave. "Let me know if you hear it again next year – that would be pretty exciting."

"I will," Maggie said, following him outside and wishing now he would stay a little longer. He paused again to look across the garden.

"I've not seen Keeper's Cottage looking this good for many years."

"Well, wait until next summer," Maggie said, her voice sparkling with enthusiasm. "I've been reading up on my plants and getting advice from the gardeners. You'll see even more of a difference. And I want to get some chickens – although Jack insists they would wreck the garden, so I'll have to make some sort of enclosure."

George pointed to the waste ground beyond the top of the garden. It was closed in on three sides by metal railings like the garden, but open on the side running by the old track to the lost bridge, the fence long gone. "Why don't you use some of that rough ground? The cattle and sheep seldom find their way in to graze it off. It would put it to good use."

Maggie was startled by the suggestion. "Do you think I could?"

"Let me run it past Richard, but I'm sure it will be fine."

Maggie didn't know what to say. It was such a generous and unexpected offer.

"Thank you so much. I do appreciate it." She looked at him and for a second all her reserve and shyness fell away. "I mean, I appreciate everything – you will never know how much."

George smiled as he climbed into his car.

When he'd gone, Maggie looked out from the front room, her eyes wandering across to Langley Edge, which was now cloaked in gold and red. It was six months since she'd left Adam. What he'd done to her would never leave her, but the memory of him – his voice, his smell – was fading. She looked at the clock. Now she had much more to look forward to. Today would be her sixth date with Phil. It had taken her until now to think of them as dates and she felt no nerves, just the excitement of seeing him again. He was kind and patient and without her needing to say anything, he seemed to sense her fragility. They had exchanged no more than goodbye kisses, and there was no pressure from him for anything more. She enjoyed being with him so much, but then the anxiety would return, eating away at her and she refused to think too far into the future.

In the last week of October, George telephoned Maggie to say that she was free to use the land they had discussed in whatever way she wanted. Maggie had taken the call at her desk with both Pamela and Geraldine present. She laughed with delight as she put the receiver down and looked up to find Geraldine staring at her. She felt compelled to explain the reason for the call and as soon as she'd finished describing her plans for the piece of ground, she knew she'd made a mistake.

"How did you manage to arrange that without checking with me?" Geraldine said. She had a way of appearing even taller when she was annoyed. She stood to attention, her slender neck lengthening. Maggie could see she was angry, though the reason why escaped her.

"I'm sorry, Geraldine. It didn't occur to me to involve you – it just came up in conversation with George. He made the suggestion."

"If by 'George' you mean Mr Parkinson, the land agent, I can assure you I will be having words with him. You're here a few weeks and think you can snap your fingers and get what you want when you want it."

Maggie glanced at Pam, hoping for her to offer some words of support, something to help put the situation into perspective. Pamela studied the paper in her typewriter and said nothing.

"Come into my office," Geraldine said, walking away. Maggie followed and closed the door behind her. She felt sick.

Geraldine stood with her back to Maggie for what seemed an age. Then she swung around to face her.

"If you go behind my back again, you will regret it." Geraldine's eyes flashed and she jabbed her finger at Maggie as she spoke, the gold bracelet jangling in support. "Just who do you think you are? You would do well to remember who gave you a job here; who makes sure you've got a house at all. Do you understand that I am the only person who will ensure you have a place here?"

Maggie was frozen by the outburst. Her heart thumped in her chest. It was as though she had been transported back to the kitchen of the apartment, standing opposite Adam, clutching the table in fear. She didn't speak.

"I asked you a question."

"Yes, Geraldine, I do." Maggie's voice was a whisper.

Geraldine came up close and Maggie could smell her perfume. "Do you think anyone else here cares about you?" Maggie could feel her body begin to tremble. "You sneak about the place like a timid mouse – the workers don't know your name, and as for the family – they barely know you exist." Geraldine smirked and turned away. Seating herself behind her desk she picked up some papers.

"Get out!" she said, without looking up.

Maggie returned to her office. She was shaking and she knew the colour had drained from her face. Pam tried to look concerned, but said nothing. With trembling hands, Maggie picked up a pen and began to write, blinded by the tears she refused to let fall.

The room wasn't as full as usual and there was less smoke in the air. Even so, Maggie could feel the strange atmosphere of the inn weighing on her; the beams, the stone-flag floors, the misshapen walls, all seeming to remind her of something she had lost or forgotten. She looked around, half expecting to see the mysterious man again, but all she saw were the now familiar faces of Langley workers. Anne came over with the drinks and sat next to Maggie.

"You can't let one person ruin everything for you."

"I know. I want to stand up to her. I want to tell her not to speak to me like that, but she has too much power over everyone. Even you said that." Maggie fought to hold back the tears that had threatened all day, but now they cascaded down her pale face. "She could take everything away from me without so much as a second's thought. And she would. She would take my job and my house just for the spite of it."

Anne reached over and placed a hand over Maggie's. "Listen, don't give up. Try to keep handling her as you have been doing. You never know, there could be the chance of a different job here in the future."

Maggie shook her head. "No, she would see to it that I worked for her or not at all. And anyway, I make too many mistakes – I never told you but I really messed up on the stocktake. I'm just not clever enough. I've got no qualifications. To be honest, I don't know how I got the job in the first place." She looked up, her grey eyes filled with sadness and worry. "This was my chance for a new start… If you knew what my life had been like before…" Her gentle weeping turned to a sob and one or two people turned to look towards them.

"Why don't you tell me?" Anne said, moving her position to protect Maggie from prying eyes. "Just talking about it might make a difference – you know you can trust me."

"I know I can." Maggie took a deep breath and dabbed at her face with a hanky, hoping not too many had seen her making a fool of herself. For a moment she thought of telling Anne about Adam, about how much she had lost. But she didn't want to. It was as if mentioning his name out loud would somehow let him into her new life. "No, it doesn't matter – the past is gone. I have to look forward – after all, I've got you, I've got Phil. My life is so good."

"Exactly, and you should be enjoying it instead of worrying about losing it."

"I know you're right, but sometimes… and I'm ashamed to say it – Geraldine scares me. Not for my life." Maggie's trembling lips turned up a fraction. "I don't think she's a murderer or anything like that."

"It wouldn't surprise me if she was," Anne said, trying to maintain a serious expression.

"It's what she can take away from me. There's something about this place that is special to me. And it's as if Geraldine knows it and is holding it over me."

"Well," Anne said, "I've got a suggestion. What about you do some home studies? You said you didn't achieve much at school – well, how about putting that right?"

It was something that had never occurred to Maggie. "Do you think I could?"

"Of course you could. Why don't you start by brushing up on the basics and then go for some sort of business studies. The dragon need never know anything about it."

It was the kind of influence that had been missing from Maggie's life since the death of her mother. She was thrilled that someone thought she was capable of improving herself.

As Maggie drove home, she found herself feeling unexpectedly cheerful; buzzing with excitement at Anne's suggestion. She would research what courses were available to do from home and get started as soon as possible. If the worst happened and she had to leave Langley, at least she would stand a better chance of a decent job elsewhere. She had to take control of her own life and put an end to others controlling it for her.

15

A Face at the Window

MAGGIE WAS ALONE IN the office looking over the fabric patterns that had been sent by the company that was to design new seating for the restaurant. She knew the one she would choose – the colours were muted and natural and would be a perfect fit with the old stables building. But it was of course Geraldine's decision along with Christina Handley and they would no doubt go for something very different. Maggie sighed and placed the images into a file and took it through to Geraldine's desk. Geraldine hated anyone going into her office when she wasn't there, allowing her assistants to do so on the understanding that they drop off what they needed to and leave. Maggie chuckled to herself as she thought about sitting at Geraldine's desk. She could imagine opening the drawer and lighting up a cigarette, leaning back in her chair and blowing smoke towards the ceiling. Maggie had never smoked, but it was worth considering just for the devilment of it.

Her smile faded. It was as though Geraldine, wherever she was, would be able to read her thoughts. She turned to go, but a paper jutting from the corner of a file already on the desk caught her eye. It was a stock sheet. She looked around even though she knew she was alone and then opened the file. It contained the sheets from the September count. They had been signed off and stamped by the accountant and returned to Geraldine. There were more than seventy pages in total held together by green treasury tags. Maggie turned a few over at random. She could see alterations throughout initialled by Geraldine, including the mistakes Maggie had made. *So it wasn't just me that made the mistakes,* she thought. She knew she was weak to need such reassurance, but nevertheless she was relieved.

That evening Maggie sat at the kitchen table. Anne had brought her a book on grammar to help her get a head start on her course. She was surprised at how much she remembered what she'd learnt at school and wondered how she could have failed her exams. The time flew by and when her eyes grew heavy she realised that she'd studied for three hours. She stretched and yawned and Rupert jumped to his feet, his tail waving as he waited for his last walk of the day.

"Come on, Dog," Maggie said, tickled at her use of Jack's name for the lurcher. "Let's get your lead." As she stood up from the table, the atmosphere in the room changed. It felt heavy and close, like before a summer thunderstorm. Then she heard the sound. At first she wasn't sure where it was coming from and then realised it came from the end of the short hallway – from the bedroom. It was the sounds from her dream, but now she was very much awake. The distinct crunching of ashes breaking and the knocking and tapping of a metal poker on grating could be heard. Maggie remained stock still. She glanced down at Rupert who was staring at her, unperturbed by the sounds. Then the noise started to fade and break up, coming and going like poor reception on a radio. Maggie took a deep breath and stepped into the hall. The bedroom door was closed and she tiptoed towards it, one hand sliding along the wall as though it might protect her. The sound became clearer again, crunch... tap... tap... tap.

There has to be an explanation, Maggie thought, and as ridiculous as it seemed, if she opened the door to reveal a real, living person busy making a fire in her bedroom, then at that moment it would have been a satisfactory solution. She approached the door. Tap... tap... tap. For a moment, Maggie thought she would lose her nerve. Her arms felt like lead, but she placed a hand on the handle and turned it. The sound stopped. She pushed the door and stepped back as it swung open, as though expecting someone would run out. The bedroom was still and quiet. As before, the fireplace was cold, the water jug and bowl untouched on the hearth.

Something cold brushed her fingers and she leaped to one side, a high-pitched squeal forced from her lungs, making Rupert, who had pushed his nose under her hand, jump with fright.

"Sorry, boy," she said, leaning against the wall and stroking the dog for no other reason than to reassure herself. Then she grabbed her coat and hurried outside.

She walked further in the dark than usual, every now and then glancing back at the lights from the cottage shining out into the darkness. The warm glow looked welcoming, but now she shivered at the thought of going back. For the first time she felt frightened of being alone and it annoyed her. There would be an explanation, she was sure of it. Even so, she stayed out for a further hour. She watched Orion climb high above Langley Edge before she felt her nerves settling and returned to the cottage. It was the early hours of the morning before she finally fell asleep, the bedroom door open, hall light on and Rupert lying at the side of her bed.

This time Maggie could not shake off the lingering sense of unease. She decided not to tell anyone of her experience – not even Anne, whilst all the time trying to find an explanation for what she'd heard. The obvious possibility was a bird trapped in the chimney and she called George Parkinson to see if someone could check. The chimney was investigated and found to be clear with a secure grill fitted to the top. With no other explanation available there was little Maggie could do, so she kept busy and willed herself not to think any more about it.

Maggie was on route to the garden shop. She walked along the dark corridors of the manor, breathing in the now familiar scent of the old building, and looking at the paintings and tapestries on the walls as she went. There was the stillness within some parts of the manor that she had experienced nowhere else. The thick walls excluded all sound from the world outside and created an atmosphere that was timeless.

She thought of the people who, over centuries, had stood where she stood, casting their eyes over the portraits just as she did now. She pushed open the heavy oak door into the great hall, imagining that she might be greeted by noblemen and ladies, the gentle sound of medieval music playing in the background. Instead she bumped straight into Richard Handley.

During her time at Langley, Maggie had seldom spoken to him. Whenever she had seen him he was usually in the company of George or Geraldine or the farms manager, and she would hurry past so as not to disturb them. Richard was a short and gaunt-looking man with receding, faded blonde hair. He seemed considerably older than Christina and could easily be mistaken for her father. Whenever Maggie had seen him, he was dressed in the same pale tweed jacket over cream moleskin trousers. He looked every inch the country gent, except on closer inspection when the threadbare elbows of the jacket become apparent along with the dropped hem of a trouser leg.

Maggie was aware that he was on his way to a meeting with Geraldine. Her words echoed in her ears, *'The family barely know you exist'*. As he passed, he smiled and said, "Good morning." Maggie whispered a response without making eye contact.

Once outside she hurried along the paths lined by low-trimmed box trees towards the garden centre. She had reached the renovated stable block when she realised she'd forgotten some papers she needed. Muttering to herself she retraced her steps. As she hurried back through the manor, the faces of the portraits, which seemed to change every time she saw them, now smirked at her in amusement.

She eased the door open, aware that Geraldine would not want to be disturbed. The door to Geraldine's office was ajar by just two or three inches, but enough for Maggie to hear Richard Handley's deep voice.

"Well, Geraldine, I think you are going to need more help. The new business has been such a huge success and you must have someone to whom you can delegate responsibility. You can't do it all, you know."

Maggie picked up the paper she needed and crept back towards the door.

"You know I like to keep a firm hold on the reins, Richard," Geraldine said in her smooth, confident tones.

"I don't mean give up ownership – I just mean get more support. You need a senior assistant of some sort; someone who can stand in for you at meetings or see some of the suppliers, that kind of thing. Have you got anyone on your team you could promote? What about that young full-time woman of yours – what's her name? Can't she take more on for you?"

Maggie froze by the door in the momentary silence that followed.

"I hope you're joking, Richard." Geraldine's incredulous voice was pitched higher than normal. "The surest way of damaging the business would be to give that girl greater responsibility – she struggles enough as it is."

"Well, just a suggestion – I thought she was doing a good job for you, but you know her best."

"Yes, I do. Maggie is fine in an office junior sort of capacity – but that's about the best I can say for her. Some people quickly reach their limits and she has certainly found hers."

Maggie stepped into the corridor, her stomach churning, legs turning to jelly. She had suspected that Geraldine would talk about her like that, but hearing her saying the words – criticising her to Richard Handley – it was more than Maggie could bear. She wanted to charge into the office and confront her there and then in front of Mr Handley. To tell him Geraldine was wrong and that she didn't deserve to be treated like that. But that would have taken the kind of courage and strength she knew she didn't possess. Instead, she walked out into a driving autumn shower, the rain hiding her tears.

"That's it," said Phil. It was a statement of completion, as he viewed his work. The rough piece of ground beyond the garden had been fenced in and a small wooden henhouse placed beneath the horse-chestnut tree.

"This is great," Maggie said. "I couldn't have done it without you. I can't wait to get the chickens – I'm fetching them from Jack later."

"All we need now is for that boss of yours to come by and see your expanding empire. It would be worth it just to see the look on her face."

Maggie had told Phil about Geraldine. She had resisted until now because talking about her always made Maggie feel pathetic. But she had been so upset by Geraldine's outburst over the land and then by what she'd said to Richard

Handley, that Maggie had confided in Phil. She had feared that he would see her as weak, but he had been nothing but supportive and reassuring. He took a similar stance to Anne – that the best way to tackle a bully like Geraldine was to get on and enjoy life, and be seen to enjoy life.

Phil came over and wrapped strong arms around her. "You are now officially a country girl," he said, as Maggie tried to wriggle away.

"You are filthy."

"Since when did a bit of dirt bother a country girl?" He planted a kiss on her lips and then looked at his watch. "I'd better get going. I need a shower before rugby."

Maggie raised her eyebrows. "Save time – don't bother showering BEFORE playing rugby."

She waved Phil off and then drove over to the Petersons, taking Rupert with her. She had visited them several times since she'd moved out and Irene was always delighted to see her.

"Jack," Irene called as she came out from the kitchen, drying her hands on her apron, "she's here and Rupert, too." There was no sign of Jack.

Irene embraced Maggie in a firm hug and patted the fussing dog.

"It's good to see you, lovely. How are things? How's that young man of yours?" Maggie had mentioned Phil on her last visit. She hoped that Irene would now stop pestering her about needing a man in her life. Of course Irene had been delighted. It created an order she considered essential for a happy existence.

"He's fine thanks, Irene. He helped me with the enclosure for the chickens today."

"Good — you make sure you hang onto him. He sounds like a good one."

"He is."

Jack appeared around the corner of the building carrying a box and followed by several dogs. He nodded at Maggie, a fleeting, toothless grin crossing his face.

"Got some good layers for you 'ere," he said. "Look after 'em and they'll produce enough for you, even at this time of year."

"This is great. You must come over and see where they will live."

"Oh, we haven't been over t' manor for a good time, have we, Jack? We should go," Irene said. Maggie had invited them several times since she'd moved, but they hadn't made it yet.

"Aye, we'll make t' journey some time," said Jack, as if the trip would take them to a foreign land.

By the time Maggie had eaten the customary meal with Jack and Irene and finally made it home, it was late afternoon when she released the chickens into their new enclosure. She watched them for an hour as they explored their new surroundings. Once the six red hens had checked out the fenced boundaries and realised they could go no further, they started to scratch about among the brown and yellow leaves. Maggie smiled with satisfaction as she watched them. She hoped Geraldine really would come by.

As dusk fell, she filled the seed tray and water container and shut the chickens into their new house. Satisfied they were safe, she walked Rupert out into the park to the front of the cottage where she stood and watched him stroll around. It was a still evening and mild for the end of October. The evening air was scented with damp soil and the musky smell of decaying leaves. Even the bats had abandoned hibernating and flitted about between the trees.

Suddenly, Maggie's skin prickled and she shivered as she turned to look at the cottage in the dimming light. The man stared back at her from inside. For a moment she thought her heart would stop. He was standing close to the glass of the middle of the three windows. She could see the strands of grey hair hanging almost to his shoulders, the dark stubble covering his gaunt face. He looked haggard – perhaps ill, but above all he exuded a deep sorrow. Maggie stared for several seconds as the figure looked back at her. He did not move at all, not even a blink in his desolate eyes. Maggie felt a confused mix of fear along with the urge to reach out towards him; to somehow comfort him. She dragged her gaze away and as she did, panic surged up inside her. She stared, wide-eyed, along the footpath, hoping someone might be walking in the park. There was no one. In alarm she turned back to the window. He was gone.

Maggie realised she wasn't breathing. She felt light-headed and bent down to let the blood to her head, calling Rupert to her in a weak, breathless voice. She recognised the man. She had seen him before, on the footpath and in the inn, but now she felt that somehow she actually *knew him*. Rooted to the spot, she stared into the cottage. Only her reflection gazed back. She knew there was no intruder in the house, that when she went back inside there would be no one there, and yet for what seemed an age she could not move.

Minutes went by – Maggie had no idea how long – before she plucked up the courage to go into the cottage, dragging Rupert with her. She dashed to the kitchen, snatched up the telephone and with trembling fingers dialled Anne's number. Maggie listened to the ringing tone, begging Anne to pick up. She held Rupert hard against her leg and stared into the hallway towards the living room. At last there was the sound of the receiver being lifted.

"Anne, thank God you're in. You've got to come. Please hurry."

16

Haunted by the Past

BY THE TIME ANNE arrived it was seven o'clock and dark but for the light of a pale half-moon. Maggie sat huddled on the garden seat, Rupert lying by her feet. As Anne's car pulled to a halt, Maggie ran to meet her.

"What's wrong? You scared me to death," Anne said.

"I've seen him again," Maggie said, grasping her friend by the arms.

"Seen who?" For a second, Anne was confused and then she comprehended what Maggie meant. "What – you mean the man?"

"Yes – right here inside the cottage." Maggie pulled her coat tightly about herself. Despite the mildness of the evening she was shivering.

"Oh my God – are you sure?" Anne said, following Maggie back to the seat, and glancing anxiously at the cottage, which stood in darkness but for the moonlight reflecting in the windows.

"I'm certain. For weeks now I've thought it was me; that I might be seeing and hearing things, but not after today. Today, I'm telling you, I saw him as clearly as I'm seeing you. He was standing in the living room staring out of the window. He was looking right at me." Maggie shuddered at the memory.

Anne sat beside her in astonished silence for several moments. The stillness of the night was only broken by the call of a tawny owl close by followed by a response from across the park.

"Blimey, Maggie, I never thought the man you saw on the footpath would be connected to the cottage."

"Nor did I – not until I heard him inside. I told myself there would be another explanation. But there isn't one." She looked at her friend, her expression a mixture of fear with bewilderment. "Keeper's Cottage really is haunted."

They sat huddled together as Maggie related her experiences; of the man calling the name Mary, of the whispered voice by her ear, and the sounds of a fire being made.

"Why on earth didn't you tell me?" Anne asked. "Did you think I wouldn't believe you?"

"I barely believed myself." Maggie pulled Rupert to her and hugged his warm body, her fingers plucking at his rough coat. "Honestly, Anne – I thought I was going mad. I sometimes wonder if I still am."

"I don't think so." Anne's smile was visible in the gloom as she tried to lighten the moment. "I told you, I believe there are many things we don't fully understand in this world and some of us are more tuned in than others. You're one of the lucky ones."

"Well, I don't feel lucky, and anyway..." Maggie hesitated.

"Come on, spit it out," Anne urged.

"I haven't told you everything. I saw him in the Stag, too. He was standing by the fire resting against the mantelpiece. I glanced away and he'd vanished. That's what happened today, too; one second he was there and the next, gone."

Maggie could feel Anne studying her face, waiting.

"It's so weird, Anne, but I feel as though I know him. I've seen him three times now and tonight he was so close. I'm sure I know him from somewhere, but I can't place him. And when I see him, I'm scared, but then another part of me wants to go to him... feels sorry for him. He looks so wretched."

Maggie gazed over her shoulder at the cottage and to the park and hillside beyond, now lost in the dark. "I don't know what it is, but I have the most peculiar feeling about this place — the cottage, the park, the inn..." She was about to mention the oak tree, but stopped herself.

"Well, you've seen him, whoever he is, on the path and in the inn, too. Perhaps it's not the cottage he's haunting, but you." The moment Anne said it, she appeared to regret it. "I'm sorry, Maggie, I didn't mean to scare you more."

"Don't worry, I'd already thought it," Maggie said, trying to be flippant, but she was already frightened that Anne was right.

"Well, what do we do now?"

"Will you go inside with me?"

Anne jumped to her feet. "Of course I will," she said, leading the way. "There really is nothing to be scared of." There was a tremor in her voice and Maggie wondered which of them she was trying to convince.

The heating was on inside the cottage and the same welcoming warmth Maggie remembered when she'd first entered the building met them now as they opened the door. They walked from room to room, switching on the lights as they went, Rupert following behind. The cottage was silent and peaceful.

Two mugs of hot chocolate later and Maggie started to warm up. She and Anne were sitting together at the kitchen table.

"Have you told Phil about what's been happening?" Anne asked.

"No – and I don't intend to," Maggie said firmly, and then forced a smile. "I can just about cope with you thinking I'm some kind of oddball, but not Phil – or at least not yet." The smile vanished. "I love the cottage so much. I've never been happier in my life, but now... it really is starting to scare me."

Maggie stared around the kitchen, her eyes wide as though she didn't know the place. The only sound came from the drip of the tap and the hoot of the owl outside. She got up and jerked the curtain across the window as though at any moment the face of the man might appear at the glass.

"Come on, Maggie, try not to be frightened," Anne said. "I just don't think, whatever it is, that it can harm you. I tell you what, why don't we try and find out more about the history of the cottage? It would be exciting to find out about who's lived here before. If the man is connected to the cottage, we might even find out who he is – was." Her eyes twinkled as she spoke.

Anne's optimism began to rub off on Maggie and her anxiety eased. Perhaps she was taking it too seriously. After all, she knew too well that it was the living that hurt you.

"I suppose it would be interesting to do a bit of investigating."

"There's no suppose about it. Let's get started straight away."

Anne offered to stay the night, but Maggie, her nerves calmed, politely declined. She was determined not to be afraid of the cottage she loved. She read until she became drowsy and then fell asleep with the lights turned on.

Her small hand felt around the edges of the wooden horse as she had done so many times before. She stroked its pointed ears and ran her fingers along the rough, carved tail. The tip of one foot had long since snapped off but the break had been rubbed smooth by her touch. She clutched it to her. It was the most precious thing in the world, but for this she was willing to part with it. She cried as she placed it into the box.

By the morning, Maggie had forgotten the dream.

The next day, Phil came over with Bracken. She was overjoyed to see him, but her pale face and dark circles beneath her eyes weren't lost on him. He held her face in his hands and brushed her hair back.

"You look like you've been up all night. Are you okay?"

"I'm fine. I just didn't sleep well for some reason. I'm all the better for seeing you."

"And how is my favourite girl – the fat one with the feathers and big feet?"

Maggie chuckled; of course, he hadn't seen the new arrivals. So much had happened since she'd collected the chickens, it seemed an age ago.

"They are all fat and they all have big feet. I think the feathers go without saying. Come on – let's go and see them."

After the mild evening, the dawn of the first of November had brought with it a sharp frost. Maggie filled the feeders and threw some seed out across the ground for the chickens to find. She stood by Phil, watching as the hens scratched about amongst the frozen leaves. She leaned against him and felt his arms close around her. She felt safe and comforted and the remaining fears from the night before evaporated.

"I tell you what, let's ring Geraldine and get her down here to look at your farmstead. Let's tell her you're having goats, too." Phil's face was serious but his eyes shone with mischief.

"Don't you dare – she hates me enough as it is."

He squeezed her hard. "Who could hate you? And anyway, I'll bet she's just a big cuddly teddy bear."

Maggie turned and beat him in mock attack until he surrendered. Then, as she turned her back, he threw an arm full of frosty leaves at her. Maggie shrieked and ran off, the chickens clucking furiously as they scampered out of the way. Bracken and Rupert joined in the fun, the scruffy terrier chasing the lurcher as fast as her short legs could carry her. Maggie was in fits of giggles when Phil caught up with her and pulled her back close to him.

"Talking of big cuddly teddy bears," he said.

Maggie rested against his chest. "Hey, watch who you're calling big."

"I was meaning me." Phil lowered his mouth to hers. The kiss was gentle and lingering.

"I don't want to leave today," he whispered. "I want to stay here with you."

"I want you to stay, too." She looked into his face, taking in every detail. The twist in the hair of his eyebrow that refused to lie flat, the small scar on his chin that still bore the stitch marks on either side, the bruise on his cheek from yesterday's match, his kind brown eyes brimming with anticipation. This time there was no self-conscious urge to look away. Taking his hand, she led him towards the cottage.

In the hallway she stopped and kissed him again. Her fingers traced the contours of his face; he hadn't shaved and she loved the feel of the stubble along his jaw. His hands were gentle on her body and his kiss was slow and measured. There was no urgency; it was as though he had all the time in the world. She eased away from him and led him towards the bedroom.

"Maggs, are you sure about this? You have to be ready."

"I am." It was all she said.

They made love, and for the first time in her life Maggie understood the meaning of the words. She'd only ever had sex with Adam. That's what it had been for three years; sometimes willingly and sometimes not, but every time it had been an act for Adam's gratification. Since those horrific last two times, when he had forced himself on her and then she had opened herself to him willingly in a desperate attempt to stay safe, the mere thought of intercourse had made her shudder. She had doubted she would ever want a physical relationship again. But now – now it was different and it was wonderful.

They spent the remainder of the day, walking and talking, blissful in each other's company. And that night they made love again and in the morning Maggie woke to find her body peacefully entwined with the man she knew she had fallen in love with.

As much as they wanted to stay where they were, in the warmth of the bed and each other, Phil had to leave for work. Maggie took Rupert for an extra-long walk and she hummed to herself as she strolled. When she reached a point where she could look down on Keeper's Cottage, she wanted to sing out loud for joy. She had discovered her paradise and now she had found someone to share it with. Nothing could spoil her joy today – even Geraldine, who was away for a week, could not ruin her happiness.

Maggie and Anne wasted no time looking into the history of Keeper's Cottage. They already knew it wasn't that old when compared to the medieval manor house. The lodge had been built in the 1840s, 500 years after the manor. Their first approach was to try and discover who had lived there during that time. Anne suggested they approach Stephen Clarke, the estate curator.

Stephen had been recruited when Richard Handley had taken over the running of Langley. As a boy, raised in the manor, Richard had always been aware of attic rooms filled with historical records; books, papers and ledgers of all kinds. Generations of his ancestors and those of the previous owners had been enthusiastic hoarders, though it appeared each with declining orderliness. As the mass of records grew, so the job of sorting them had become ever more daunting. When Richard returned to Langley, he knew there would be historical importance to some of the records, and decided that the only way to tackle the huge task was to employ someone to sort and record everything. That was Stephen Clarke's job.

He was a quiet, studious man who kept to himself and Maggie had never spoken to him. He was old-fashioned and could have stepped from the history books he researched. Everything about him appeared dated; his clothes, hair, spectacles, all belonged to another time and situated in the unaltered attic rooms, he fitted his surroundings perfectly. Maggie sometimes passed him on the long corridors and he always looked to be one step away from breaking into a jog and far too busy to speak. His constantly harassed manner suggested he had little time for trivia, and now, as Anne and Maggie knocked at his door, Maggie worried that they would be wasting his time.

"You'd be surprised how many requests I get regarding the history of Langley and its people – even from abroad. It seems those who research their family trees are attracted to stately homes. I think it's in the hope of discovering some lost aristocratic connections," Stephen said with strained humour. He was standing by his desk, which was the only clear space in his office. It stood like an island in a sea of rolled documents, old books, and loose papers. Maggie and Anne stayed by the door as it was almost impossible to enter without stepping on something.

"Well, at least we aren't trying to trace any particular family, just information about Keeper's Cottage. Anything at all about it would be useful to us, Stephen," Anne said in bright, confident tones. "We realise you are extremely busy, but we would be so grateful."

For a moment, Maggie thought her friend's charm was working as, taking a deep breath and pushing his spectacles back up his nose he scanned around the room as though looking for something that might be useful. She was disappointed.

"It wouldn't be so bad if I had anything from that time recorded. Mr Handley is particularly interested in the early history of Langley, so I'm afraid I'm concentrating on the older items first and working my way forward. All I can say is, if I come across something that might be of interest to you, I'll let you know."

Maggie was deflated, but tried to hide it. "Thank you for your time, Mr Clarke. We really do appreciate it."

They turned to leave and Stephen called after them. He tiptoed his way across the paper-strewn floor.

"Someone you might want to talk to – Fred Walcott. He's a retired chap who lives in Bransby. I remember talking to him once and I'm sure he mentioned that he'd lived at

Keeper's Cottage for a few years when he was younger." He turned back into his office. "Perhaps he's as good a starting point as any."

That lunchtime, Maggie drove home to let Rupert out for a run. It had turned into a grey, drizzly day and there were few visitors around. As she walked with the dog, she wondered if Stephen would ever get back to them.

The drizzle turned to steady rain and Langley Edge disappeared behind a veil of low cloud. Maggie pulled her wax hat firmly down as she hurried along. A few hundred yards ahead of her, a couple were walking across the wet grass and onto the road towards the manor. There was something about the man that caught her attention. He was tall and long-legged and strode out in a nonchalant way, but fast enough that the woman with him had to jog now and again to keep up. As Maggie strained her eyes to focus through the rain, a nauseating sensation came over her and she stopped in her tracks. It looked like Adam.

Her legs felt as though they had weights tied to them as she ran back to the cottage. *Surely it can't be him. But what if it is? Even if it his him, that doesn't mean he knows I'm here. No, it won't be him. But I have to know.* If she could just get back to her car and drive closer, then she would know.

Pushing Rupert into the cottage, she leapt into her car. Her hands shook so violently she struggled to get the key into the ignition. She drove quickly towards the manor and saw that the couple had just arrived at a parked car in the distance. A car she didn't recognise. She braked hard, bringing the vehicle to a halt in the middle of the road. She breathed a sigh of relief. It wasn't his car. *But what if he's changed it? What if it's the woman's?* She dared not go closer. The vehicle pulled out of its parking space and was driven away at speed, disappearing in the distance.

17

The Paintings

MAGGIE WAS STILL SHAKEN as she walked to her office. She tried to persuade herself that the man she'd seen couldn't have been Adam. There was no reason for him to be there; unless her father had told him. She felt sick again. Although she hadn't seen her father since she'd left, he had her address. Surely if he'd had contact with Adam and told him where she was, he would have made himself known by now – he wouldn't be able to help himself. The thoughts continued to swirl around her head as she pushed her door open.

"Mrs Handley wants to see you," Pam said, before Maggie had even stepped into the room. She was trying to sound matter of fact through thinly disguised envy.

"She wants to see me? Why?" Maggie was breathless as she spoke.

"She didn't say – you'd better go and find out." Pam didn't look at her as she spoke.

Maggie quickly combed her hair, which looked limper than ever from the rain, and tried to compose herself as she hurried through the manor. She knew where Christina Handley's private sitting room was, but she had never been inside. She tapped on the door and waited.

"Come in – is it Maggie?"

Christina Handley was sitting at a large table in the centre of the room. Eddie, the black Labrador, was stretched out on his side underneath. Spread across the table was a selection of colour photographs of paintings. Christina was on the telephone and she beckoned Maggie forward whilst she continued speaking.

Maggie stayed by the door, nervously fiddling with her fingers behind her back. The room was comfortable and pretty. The walls were painted in duck-egg blue and the furniture had soft coverings of pinks and greys. Paintings of dogs intermingled with photographs of classic cars covered the walls and numerous family photographs stood on the mantelpiece and writing desk.

Christina ended her telephone conversation and saw Maggie looking at a photograph of an E-type Jaguar.

"Those are from when I was much younger. Not many people know of my interest in cars."

"I'm sorry, Mrs Handley, I didn't mean to be intrusive."

"I'm pleased for you to see them. They remind me of a time before I met Richard – before all this." She gestured with her hands to mean the manor and a hint of sadness crossed her face. Maggie didn't know how old she was but guessed she wasn't much older than thirty. It was the first time it had occurred to Maggie how daunting a thing it was to marry into such heritage and to be saddled with the responsibility of running a place like Langley.

"Anyway, thank you for coming down, Maggie, I understand Geraldine is away."

For a moment, Maggie was taken aback that Christina was speaking to her as though she knew her. They had barely spoken before.

"Yes, she is… for the week. I think she has business in London." Maggie knew she sounded timid and wasn't sure why she felt the need to explain Geraldine's absence.

"Yes, well, these have been painted by Charlotte Green, a good friend of mine," Christina said, casting her hand over the images on the table. She looked up, smiling. "Come on over and take a look at them. Aren't they striking?"

Maggie moved closer and looked at the small photographs of oil landscapes. They looked impressive, although she would not have considered herself any judge of art.

"They're beautiful."

"Aren't they? I would like to hang a few of the originals in our kitchen tea room. What do you think?"

"I think they would look wonderful," Maggie said, blushing and wondering why Christina would be interested in what she thought.

"Right," Christina said enthusiastically, "pull up a chair and let's decide which ones we want."

Maggie hesitated. The panic she'd felt less than thirty minutes before had barely subsided; now she felt it rising again.

"Do you think it might be better to wait until Geraldine comes back next week, Mrs Handley; let her choose with you?"

"No, not at all. I told Charlotte I had room for six and she's visiting in a few days and can bring them with her." She looked directly at Maggie who was aware for the first time of her striking grey-blue eyes. They were piercing and at the same time exuded gentleness. "Come on, Maggie," Christina said, pointing across the room, "bring that chair over and let's decide."

For the next half hour, they went over the copies of eighteen oil paintings. For the entire time, Maggie wondered why Christina had asked her opinion. She could have asked anyone — or no one, as she didn't really need help at all.

Christina picked her favourites and on the whole Maggie agreed that they were a good selection and felt relieved that she wouldn't have to disagree. But her eye was constantly drawn to one overlooked moorland painting of grouse flying against rain-laden clouds.

"Which is your favourite?" Christina asked surveying the selected six.

Maggie pushed a strand of limp hair behind her ear, embarrassed. "It is actually one we haven't chosen."

"Well, why not? Which one is it?"

Maggie pointed to the moorland scene and Christina examined it.

"Which of the ones we have picked do you like the least?" Maggie drew forward the one that, if she was honest, was more suited to a chocolate box.

"That's it then," Christina announced. "The decision is made. That one is out and yours is in. I will let Charlotte know without delay."

Maggie had relaxed in the presence of this charming woman; she was so easy to talk to. "They would make wonderful prints. We could put them in the interiors section of the shop. I'm sure they would sell," she said.

No sooner were the words out of her mouth, than she regretted them. She had no right to be so forward.

"Well, I had only thought of displaying the paintings. Charlotte doesn't normally sell her work, you understand."

"No, of course... it was just a thought that came to mind, Mrs Handley. I shouldn't have mentioned it."

"I appreciate your views and I think your idea is a good one. I will ask Charlotte to consider it. Thank you for helping me with this, Maggie, I have enjoyed our time together."

Maggie walked back through the manor, the warm glow inside her dissipating with every stride. It was such a small thing to be involved in, and she was thrilled that Christina had asked her (though the reason why evaded her), but she knew she would pay if Geraldine found out. Try as she might, the brief sense of satisfaction began to turn to dread.

Fred Walcott's cottage was semi-detached, with mullioned windows and a tiny garden to the front. A leafless thorny rose clambered over the door. It was like many of the houses in Bransby and exactly the kind she'd imagined she might have been offered. The unique Keeper's Cottage had been way beyond her expectations.

They sipped tea in Fred's front room, sitting by the small leaded window that looked out over the roofs of the village. Fred was a short, plump man with a red face, and he loved to talk. He was delighted to have a visitor and especially one that was interested in the past. If Maggie had thought the conversation might be difficult, she need not have feared. When it came to banter, Fred was the opposite of Jack. He proved to be a fountain of knowledge about the Langley estate and the people who'd lived and died there in his time. Most importantly he knew who had lived at Keeper's Cottage for some years before he had. But he was so enjoying talking to her about Langley – what it used to be like and how much it had changed – that it took some time, and three cups of tea, before she could coax him back to the subject of the cottage.

"You were going to tell me about when you lived at Keeper's Cottage," Maggie prompted.

"Well, me and my Molly moved there in '49. That was after Mrs Kersey died. She had the worst case of tuberculosis I ever saw. But, I tell you this, it took a long while before it put her in her grave." Fred got up with an effort and limped to the kitchen to fetch the kettle and poured more boiling water into the teapot.

"Did she have a husband, Mrs Kersey?"

"Oh aye, she did, but he was killed during the war – the first war. Bit of a sad story. He was only about thirty and they never had a family." He poured another cup of tea for himself and offered one to Maggie.

"No thank you, Fred. You were saying…"

"Well, she never married again and by all accounts she became a bit of a recluse down there by the marshes. Anyway, after she passed, me and Molly – she's been gone more than ten years now – moved in and we stayed for about five years." The old man's eyes misted a little as he thought back to long years with his wife. He took a sip from his cup and carried on. "After us, there was various folk lived there for a while, but they moved on when they had youngsters. It's not big, is it?"

Maggie smiled. "Not for a growing family, no, it isn't."

"Do you know who lived there before Mrs Kersey?"

"No I don't – that was well before my time."

"What was the cottage like to live in when you were there?"

"Well, it was fair enough – for a while. But once our second came along – well, it wasn't big enough. But I tell you what sticks in my mind most about that place..."

Maggie leaned forward in anticipation.

"It was that roof. Never could stop the damn thing leaking. I tell you, love, we was never warm the whole time we lived in it. I suppose it's got some new-fangled central heating in it now?"

"Yes it has – well, ugly looking storage heaters. But it's really cosy now and it's got a nice new kitchen – you should call in for a look."

"I'd like that."

Maggie had taken enough of the old man's time and rose from her chair. "Thank you so much for sharing your memories. I've learned a lot more about the cottage and about the estate for that matter."

"How do you like living at Keeper's Cottage then?" Fred asked.

Maggie suspected he was trying to delay her leaving.

"Oh, I love it," she said with easy enthusiasm. "From the moment I stepped into the place it felt special – they've even fixed the roof."

Fred chuckled. "And what about being so close to them marshes?"

"It's wonderful – I love the birds. I was talking to George Parkinson. I told him I heard something that he said sounded like a bittern, but he thought it was unlikely."

"Aye, George is right. I know my birds and there hasn't been a bittern there for a long time. I can remember my grandfather telling me there was once a time when those reed beds was full of them, but not anymore."

Maggie stepped outside into a biting north wind. "Perhaps I was just lucky enough to hear one that was just passing through."

Fred looked at her doubtfully. "Aye, maybe so."

It had been an interesting two hours with Fred, though his information about the cottage had revealed nothing that helped her. She had one last try.

"Fred, did you ever experience anything... strange or odd while you lived at Keeper's Cottage?"

Fred gave her a curious look. "I'm not sure what you mean, but no. The oddest thing I remember about that place was how that damned roof could still leak no matter how many times you fixed it!"

With that, the conversation was over.

Geraldine returned the following week and to the relief of everyone, especially Maggie, she seemed to be in good spirits. This lasted until Wednesday. Christina Handley had returned from a few days away and had summoned Geraldine to the café in the old kitchens.

Geraldine stood next to Maggie's desk, standing over her. "For some reason she wants you to come with me."

Maggie's heart skipped a beat. This was what she had dreaded and she doubted anything she said would help, but perhaps if she tried to forewarn Geraldine, it might help.

"I'm not sure... but it might be the paintings she mentioned last week." Her voice sounded hoarse.

"What paintings? Why didn't you tell me?"

"I never thought. It was nothing, just a quick chat about some paintings from one of Mrs Handley's friends."

"Well, we'd better go and see what has materialised from that quick chat." Geraldine marched out and Maggie hurried after her, noticing the faintest glimmer of a smirk on Pam's face as she passed her desk.

As the manor was now only open to visitors at weekends until Christmas, there was no one in the kitchen café as they arrived, apart from Christina Handley and a workman.

"Ah, Geraldine, it's good to see you. Did you have successful meetings last week?"

"Yes, I saw a few new suppliers for next year – I think you will be pleased with what I have planned for the garden centre." To Maggie it sounded as though she didn't care if Christina liked her ideas or not.

"Oh, that's good. Now let me show you these paintings by my friend Charlotte. Don't you think they will look stunning in here?" She cast her eye along the bare stone wall on the opposite side to the cooking range. "I think they will add some colour, don't you?"

Maggie held her breath, praying that Christina wouldn't implicate her.

"To be honest, Christina, no, I think they are quite awful."

Maggie was aghast. To see how Geraldine could speak to Christina like that in front of others and remain completely unruffled whilst doing so astounded her. Anyone coming in at that moment would have assumed that Geraldine was the owner and Christina Handley no more than her assistant.

"Oh, I'm sorry to hear that," Christina said, a pink flush coming to her face. "What is it about them you don't like?"

"I think they are garish, and completely out of place for a room like this."

Maggie froze. Geraldine was able to criticise Christina's taste in style as well as her friend's artistic abilities in one easy sentence. She willed Christina to stand her ground.

Christina took a deep breath and surveyed the empty wall. "Well, John is here ready to start hanging, and Maggie and I spent a good deal of time deciding which ones to take, so I think we should give them a try. I'm sure you have more important things to be doing, Geraldine, perhaps Maggie should stay and help me decide where to put them."

Geraldine glared at Christina for a split second and then walked, stony-faced, from the kitchen. Maggie knew she was in trouble.

18

Caught Out

Maggie and Christina stood together surveying the empty kitchen wall, whilst John positioned the hooks. Christina appeared to have recovered from the discomfort of Geraldine's remarks and turned her attention back to the paintings with renewed enthusiasm. All that needed to be done now was to decide the order in which they should hang. Several variations were tried with Christina seeking Maggie's opinion each time and the ever-patient John swapping and changing the paintings as requested. For Maggie, that hour, during which her opinion was sought and heeded, was both satisfying and motivating. Only when it was over did she begin to worry about what was in store for her once she returned to the office.

She trudged dejectedly back through the manor, the energy she'd felt minutes before evaporating. Her legs felt heavy as though rebelling against the direction in which she walked. She tried to think of what she would say; that it wasn't her fault; that Mrs Handley had simply asked her opinion; that if Geraldine had been around it wouldn't have happened at all. Every response seemed certain to annoy Geraldine further.

Pam carried on typing as Maggie entered the room and said nothing. There was no sound from the adjoining room. After several minutes, and unable to withstand the tension any longer, Maggie spoke.

"Is Geraldine in?"

"No," Pam said. "She called in half an hour ago, took her bag and went straight out."

Maggie watched Pam closely. "Did she say anything?"

"Not a word."

The afternoon dragged by and Geraldine didn't return. For the first time at Langley, Maggie watched the clock. At dead on five o'clock she left the building. She drove home and sat in the car looking at Keeper's Cottage. She felt tired and her head ached, a relentless pressure above her eyes. It was already dark and the November rain, which had set in a week ago with barely a break, now fell steadily. Maggie didn't care, she couldn't face sitting alone in the cottage. She changed her clothes and took Rupert out into the gloom of the park. She walked slowly along the footpath leading away from the manor and then worked her way around in an arc, over Heron Brook. After an hour, she still could not bring herself to return to the lonely cottage and instead continued on the road leading back to the manor.

Her head still pounded as she walked and she could feel tension clawing at her stomach. It was hard to believe that only a few days before she'd lain in Phil's arms, experiencing happiness she'd never known. Now all she felt was the heavy burden of fear weighing her down. It was a sensation she knew well and something she'd tried hard to leave behind, but now it returned, creeping its way into every part of her life. There had been the visions and sounds of the strange man. There was Geraldine, powerful and paranoid, and a constant threat to her new life. And there was Adam. She was still unsure if it had been him she'd seen. She had resisted contacting her father, frightened of finding out for certain that Adam knew where she was. Now it seemed the not knowing was worse than facing the truth. And then there was Phil. She loved him, but the closer they became, the nearer it brought her to having to reveal things she wished she could hide forever.

She stopped and stared into the parkland, now a black void.

She hadn't intended to get pregnant, and yet somewhere, in her innocence, Maggie had thought it was fate. That somehow it would soften Adam, bring the best out in him. Make things better.

A strong gust of wind blew down the valley and Maggie turned her face into it, as though the stinging rain that mingled with her tears and froze her skin might wash away the pain.

She had waited three months and then a fourth and still she dare not tell him. At five months the pregnancy started to show and she had no choice. He accused her of trying to trap him. He said it was a ploy because he hadn't married her. Enraged, he had beaten her and thrown her out of the apartment onto the landing. When she had begged him not to hurt the baby he had dragged her by her hair and pushed her down a flight of stairs.

Even with the noise of the wind and driving rain in her face, she could hear the surgeon's voice as though he were standing by her side. 'I'm so sorry, Miss Armstrong; there was nothing we could do. You were losing too much blood from the haemorrhage. There was no alternative other than to carry out an emergency hysterectomy.' Maggie could remember her response; how ridiculous her first question had been. 'Is the baby all right, though?' Of course she wasn't all right. The tiny girl had never stood a chance.

'Your partner is devastated. He's waiting outside,' the surgeon had said.

Adam had taken care of her. He said he was sorry. That was last November, just one year ago. It had taken her weeks to recover physically. She had returned to work having had surgery for an unspecified reason. Soon after, the beatings had started again.

The day she had wanted to end it all came back to her with stark clarity. She had sat in her car and watched as the lorry approached. She had come so close. It was the day she'd found Langley. She took a deep breath and ran her fingers through her drenched hair. Standing alone in the dark, she shook her head as though issuing a defiant 'NO' to a silent question. She could not allow herself to be dragged back into the depths of despair.

The sound of two vehicles heading towards the manor cut through the wind. All Maggie could see were the pairs of headlights, which instead of stopping at the main gates to the house as she expected, continued further along the outer wall to the iron gates that led to the garden. Curiosity pushed aside her misery and calling Rupert to her, she hurried closer.

She was soon near enough to make out the garden gates opening and the larger of the two vehicles drive through. Moving closer still and staying close to the protection of a group of hawthorn trees, she could see that the vehicle remaining outside was the Triumph sports car belonging to Geraldine. Maggie, hidden from sight, watched, fascinated. Everything about what she observed seemed odd. She couldn't see her watch but guessed it must be at least seven o'clock and all the workers had long since left the manor. The only lights came from the private rooms in the north wing and the small gatehouse at the main entrance where she knew a security man would be on duty.

After twenty minutes, the large vehicle, which Maggie could now see was a van, reappeared and pulled away. The lights of the Triumph suddenly illuminated the entrance and Maggie could make out Geraldine locking the gates. Then she too drove away.

Intrigued, Maggie headed to the gatehouse. Three men took turns to cover the night shift at the manor. They came to work each day just as Maggie was leaving and she'd got to know them quite well. They wouldn't say anything to Geraldine – and even if they did, Maggie would pretend she didn't know who she'd seen.

"I hope you don't mind me mentioning, Charlie," Maggie said, leaning into the warm gatehouse, which was no more than a single guardroom, "I just thought I'd make sure you knew someone had been into the garden with a vehicle."

Charlie sat close to a small electric fire reading a newspaper. It was quite possible he hadn't seen the vehicles at all, Maggie thought.

"Aye, that's all right, Maggie. I'm always glad of an extra pair of eyes about the place – especially after dark. As it happens, it was your boss seeing in a delivery from one of her suppliers. They let her know they were running late and she arranged to let them in."

"Oh, that's all okay then. I didn't realise it was Geraldine," Maggie lied.

"Well, it does happen now and again. She must be a very patient lady, that's all I can say. I'd turn 'em away with a flea in their ear if they couldn't get here on time."

"You mean it's happened before?"

"Just two or three times, and only once as I can remember when I was on duty and that was some weeks ago – back in September, I think." He reached for a book. "We log everything down here – that's it, thirtieth of September – late stock delivery – Geraldine Walker."

Maggie smiled at Charlie. "Well, just as long as everything is okay."

"It certainly is, love, and thanks for keeping a look out. You should be getting back to your cottage out in this weather – you look soaked already."

As she walked back to Keeper's Cottage, Maggie felt better. The fresh air had done her good, but it was Geraldine's odd behaviour that had distracted her from her worries. It didn't make sense. Why would she, of all people, go out of her way to let deliveries in that were late?

The next day, Geraldine didn't show at all. If she'd left a message with Pam, it hadn't been passed on. Maggie was relieved, even if it was only delaying the inevitable verbal lashing. She went to the warehouse, which was positioned at one end of the stable block, a hundred yards from the garden centre. Two brothers in their late teens worked there and they were getting ready to move stacks of outdoor planters to the shop.

"Morning," Maggie said. "I've come down to collect the paperwork for the deliveries yesterday." She thought how silly she'd feel if they simply handed over the sheets.

"Hi, Maggie," Tim, the eldest of the two said. "Nothing yesterday."

"What about last night — I understand there was a late delivery? Geraldine saw it in?"

Tim laughed out loud as his brother sniggered. "You must be joking. You think Miss High-and-Mighty does things like that? No, this place is just as we left it; nothing new in here."

"Okay, my mistake," Maggie said lightly and hurried back to the office.

With her heart racing, she searched through Geraldine's desk for the stock sheets she'd seen a few weeks before. She hoped they were still there and they were, buried beneath catalogues. Grabbing some paper, Maggie scribbled down the items where the quantity had been reduced. Voices sounded in the corridor outside and fighting panic, she threw the file back into the drawer and slamming it shut, ran back to her own office. She closed Geraldine's office door just as the door from the corridor opened. It was Christina Handley.

"Hello, Maggie, is Geraldine around?"

"I'm sorry, Mrs Handley, no she isn't," Maggie said, trying to catch her breath.

"That's a pity. When will she be back?"

Maggie tried to think of an excuse for Geraldine's absence, but could come up with nothing but the truth.

"I'm afraid I don't know – she may have left a message but I didn't get it." It suddenly occurred to Maggie that perhaps this was an opportunity to get some support from Christina. "Actually, I think Geraldine was annoyed that I'd helped you with the paintings. She prefers to do that sort of thing herself."

"Nonsense, I'm sure she hasn't given it another thought."

Maggie's feeble attempt had backfired and she regretted saying something. It seemed that Christina had pushed Geraldine's rudeness out of her mind.

"Anyway," Christina continued, "I wanted you both to meet Charlotte."

She moved aside and a woman in her late sixties stepped into the room from the corridor. She was tall and upright, with straight grey hair tied back in a tight bun. She had a commanding presence – in some ways she looked like Geraldine might in thirty years, Maggie thought.

She surveyed Maggie with a stern face. "So you must be the young lady who thought I should have my paintings reproduced?"

Concern was written all over Maggie's face and Charlotte smiled. Her lined face, which had seen too much sun over the years, crinkled.

"Don't look so worried," she said. "I think it's a lovely idea and thank you for suggesting it. I'm more than happy to have the six paintings on display reproduced for sale."

"It was a brilliant idea," Christina chimed in, "and I'm sure Geraldine will agree. Will you let her know when you see her so that she can organise it?"

"Yes, of course," Maggie whispered.

You really have no idea, do you? she thought, as she watched the two ladies leave.

As soon as they'd gone, Maggie called Anne at the estate office.

"Can you meet me at the inn after work?"

"You beat me to it," Anne said. "I've had a call from Stephen. I've got some information for you."

"That's great," Maggie said, trying to sound enthusiastic. "But I want to talk to you about something else." She put her mouth close to the receiver and whispered, "I'm not sure what, but I think Geraldine is up to something."

19

Joseph Wells

THEY SAT IN THE corner of the inn and Maggie described the incident from the evening before. She spoke in hushed tones, making sure they couldn't be overheard. There weren't many people in the bar, but Maggie knew there would always be someone with an ear out for gossip.

"Can you think of a reason why Geraldine would let a supplier into the garden after closing time? It doesn't sound like her, does it?"

"Perhaps she was in a particularly good and helpful mood," Anne said, her voice thick with sarcasm.

"Well, let's say that's the case. How come there was no record of what had been delivered? The warehouse lads had no idea about it."

"What if she forgot to leave the paperwork? What if she took it with her by mistake and will drop it in when she comes back?" Anne took a sip of her drink, eyeing Maggie over the rim of the glass. "I'm not playing this down on purpose, Maggie, but I'm not sure what you think is happening."

"I don't think I made any mistakes in the stock count. I'm not saying I don't get things wrong, of course I do, but I couldn't understand how I'd miscounted such large pieces. I think Geraldine has taken items she knew I'd recorded. She knew how easy it would be to blame me – her useless assistant." Maggie leaned in closer to Anne. "I think she took them, and last night I think she took more."

Anne raised her eyebrows. "That would be hard to prove, Maggie. And anyway, why would she do it? She already earns more than you and I could dream of, plus a rich husband – she hardly needs to steal to kit out her mini mansion."

Maggie sighed. "I don't know, and anyway, no one would believe it."

"Perhaps George Parkinson would."

"No, I can't – not without proof. I may as well pack my bags now if I accuse her of something she hasn't done." She looked at Anne with a resigned expression. "Actually, I may as well pack my bags anyway."

She explained the saga of the paintings.

"Geraldine was irate. The odd thing is I haven't seen her since. I think she's just letting me stew, biding her time."

"Listen, now is the time to stand up to her. You've done nothing wrong."

"I know, but I don't think anyone will back me up. Even Mrs Handley seems to ignore how awful Geraldine can be. She was so rude to her yesterday; but she seems to accept it." Maggie puffed out her cheeks. "I'm telling you, Anne, if I thought Geraldine was angry before, wait until I tell her about the prints – my idea."

"Listen, cross that bridge when you come to it," Anne said, lifting her bag onto the table and rummaging inside. "I've got a bit of information that's more interesting than Geraldine Walker. Stephen has been trying to get hold of you; when he couldn't get you, he contacted me. He'd forgotten he was contacted last year by someone trying to trace their family history."

"What's the connection to Keeper's Cottage?"

"It was only when he came across the letter again yesterday that it jogged his memory." Anne sniggered. "You saw his office – he probably tripped over it. Anyway that's when he remembered that this man had already traced as far back as the 1870s and that the man's great-great-great-grandfather had lived at Keeper's Cottage. He wanted to know if Langley knew anymore."

"Well, that's going to fill in a piece of the jigsaw. Does Stephen have the details?"

"He certainly does. We have the name and address of the man researching his family and the name of the man who lived in Keeper's Cottage." Anne paused for effect. "He was the head forester and he was called Joseph Wells."

Anne's face was triumphant as she watched her friend. "I'll let you absorb that, while I get us a drink. Then we'll decide what to do next."

Maggie sat back and blew a silent whistle. "Joseph Wells," she said out loud. Instantly the atmosphere in the room changed and the weird feeling she'd experienced before in the inn enveloped her. She gazed around. The inn was quiet and no one was smoking. Everyone, apart from Anne, was seated. And yet Maggie could detect the strong smell of pipe tobacco and hear the sound of work boots on unseen feet scraping across the stone flags. A haze closed around her creating a smoky veil that separated her from Anne who chatted to the barman only a few feet away. Maggie got to her feet and, as though in a dream, walked across the room to the fireplace. Her eyes scanned the old photographs on the wall before resting on one in particular. It was the team of horses outside the inn. Her breath caught as she looked at the man leaning against the wall, pipe to his mouth, watching the stable lad unharnessing the horses.

A hand rested on her shoulder.

"Maggie?"

Maggie jumped, a hand clutching to her chest.

"Sorry," Anne said, "I was calling you, but you were miles away."

"It's him," Maggie said, pointing to the photograph. "He's been here the whole time. This is why I know him – I saw this picture the first time I came in here. I never thought to look at it again until now." She hesitated and then looking back at the image said, "It was just now, when you said the name – I felt drawn to it. I think this is Joseph Wells."

Anne moved closer. The photograph was grainy and faded, but the features of the man were clear enough. On the edge of the stained card mount around the photo was written, *Stag Inn 1870*. There were no names.

"It would be a pretty amazing coincidence. Are you sure it's him? He looks a bit healthier than you've described."

"It's him." Maggie was adamant. "He doesn't look like he does when I've seen him, but it's him. And anyway…" she turned to face Anne, "do you really think that coincidence is more amazing than the fact that I've seen someone three times who lived over a hundred years ago?"

They returned to their table and Maggie sat down, peering cautiously around the room. It had returned to normal. There was no pipe smoke or scraping of boots on the stone flags.

"Joseph Wells," Maggie said. There was something about the name, but she couldn't place what it was. "I never believed in ghosts… but now – that's what it has to be. Joseph lived at Keeper's Cottage, perhaps he loved it as much as I do and he returns now and then… you know, to his favourite places. Remember, I saw him here, too."

"I think you should write to the man who was doing the research. See if he found anything else about this Joseph Wells," Anne suggested. She was brimming with excitement. "I think I might even come and stay with you to see if I can catch a glimpse of him."

Maggie laughed. "You're loving this, aren't you? I tell you what, if you see him, you can offer him a room at your place. I'd be more than happy if he left me alone."

"I don't think Tom would be too pleased. Anyway, one mystery has been solved tonight. Now you know why you feel you know this man. You saw his photograph and that image stuck in your memory."

"That's what it's got to be," Maggie said, though somewhere in the depths of her mind, a nagging doubt remained.

That evening, Maggie composed a letter to John Charlton, the man who was tracing his family. She wrote that unfortunately she had nothing more to tell him about Joseph Wells. She thought it best not to mention she had seen him on several occasions! Instead she explained that she now lived in Keeper's Cottage and that she was interested to know more of its history and who had lived there in the past. She wondered if he could tell her anything more.

After Maggie had finished the letter, she stepped out into the darkness with Rupert and walked to the chicken enclosure. She took deep, calming breaths as she walked, shining a torch ahead. She jumped as a hedgehog hurried by with surprising speed on long legs across the track in front of her. Rupert shot after it, but quickly gave up as it rolled into prickly defence.

"Come on, Rupert, leave him alone. He should be hibernating by now," Maggie said to the dog, her voice taut with nerves.

The chickens were already locked safely inside their hut, but Maggie had seen a fox patrolling close to Keeper's Cottage and she wouldn't rest until she'd made a final check. When she was satisfied that the 'girls' were secure, she walked back to the cottage, thoughts of the past few days filling her mind. Fear and a crippling lack of confidence were beginning to consume her once more. She stopped by the gate into the garden and peered around in the darkness. Holding onto the cold metal of the gate, she closed her eyes and listened to the sounds of the night; the hedgehog rooting around not far away, the screech of an owl, and the distant yap of the fox. Holding onto the metal rails of the gate, she closed her eyes and took in slow lungs full of icy air and with each breath, peace and comfort seeped back into her mind.

On Friday afternoon, Geraldine returned to work. It was as though she hadn't been absent at all. She worked in her office, said very little to anyone, and made no mention of the paintings. Maggie fretted over telling her about the prints and then decided it would be best to do the deed as a written note – simply passing the message on from Christina.

"This is a message for you from Mrs Handley," Maggie said, with as much confidence as she could muster. She held her breath while Geraldine read it.

"It was your idea, you sort it," Geraldine said, passing the note back with not a trace of emotion.

Maggie returned to her office. What did this mean? Why wasn't Geraldine angry? Relieved and at the same time perplexed, she got on with the task of finding a printing firm to reproduce the paintings.

That evening, Phil arrived to stay for the weekend. As Maggie cuddled up to him in bed, the comfort she usually found in his presence was diminished by anxiety. Only after she had made her mind up as to what she must do, could she relax. Snuggling down she rested her head on his chest and closed her eyes. Tomorrow she would tell him.

The rain had finally stopped and Saturday morning was bright and still. They walked together hand in hand along the path to the oak. The track was thickly carpeted in sodden leaves and the smell of rotting foliage hung in the air. Delicate heads of fungi, which pushed up through the dead foliage, were snapped off as the dogs raced by.

When they reached the oak, Maggie put her hand on the trunk as she always did. The bark was wet and drops of water dripped onto her skin from the branches above. She didn't expect anything to happen. She just liked to touch the tree and imagine she could feel its living energy.

"Come on," Phil said, "I'll put my coat on the stone and we can sit for a while till we get cold."

Maggie snuggled next to him. She didn't feel nervous. She knew she must do it; she had to rid herself of the endless worry.

"I've never felt like this with anyone – ever," she said, looking down on the cottage in the distance, the ancient ridge and furrow shadows falling across on the grassland.

"I love you, too," Phil said, putting his arm around her and squeezing her tight.

She felt her heart skip. It was the first time he'd said that. She'd never said it.

The dogs disturbed a squirrel burying acorns. It darted past them in a grey blur and hurtled down the steep hillside, Rupert and Bracken in pursuit.

Phil let out one of his shrill whistles, but there was no response. "It'll be a while till we see them again," he said.

"I need to tell you something," Maggie whispered, pressing her head onto his chest so as not to look at him.

"That sounds ominous."

"No – it isn't. It's just the truth," she said, keeping her eyes locked on the cottage. "I was in a horrible relationship before I came here."

"I sort of guessed that," Phil said, his voice calm and low.

"I don't know why I stayed with him for so long – I will never know. I was always too frightened – too scared to do anything, even save myself." She felt the arm hold her tighter. "Then he went too far." She fell quiet as she battled with herself to release the words; to finally allow them out. "I was pregnant. He beat me. I lost the baby. She would have been a perfect little girl." It was the first time she'd said the truth out loud to anyone and it came in short, sharp sentences, like painful spasms. There were no words that could ever convey the pain.

"I'm so sorry, Maggie." Phil's hand brushed her hair from her forehead and he leant down and kissed her.

Maggie took a trembling breath. She couldn't stop now.

"The consultant said the haemorrhage was unusual – I was just unlucky. But I can't have children. I can never have a child of my own. I needed you to know that."

Maggie waited. Phil was silent.

At last he reached down and tilted her chin up to face him. There were tears in his eyes and she realised he had been fighting to control his own emotions. She could see anger in his face and sadness, but there was something else too; something she couldn't define.

The look vanished as he spoke. "Sweetheart, do you have any idea what a wonderful, caring, beautiful woman you are? I love you and I want to be with you. That's all I know. If you want to be with me, then when the time comes we can think about other ways of building a family. Nothing you have said alters how I feel about you."

She grasped at his neck, clinging to him. "I love you. I love you so much," she said.

Suddenly she was sobbing; uncontrolled, gasping cries rising up as they had once before by the oak tree. This time she understood why. He held her for long minutes until she was exhausted, all emotion spent. Then they were quiet again until Phil spoke.

"What's his name?"

"No." Her voice was hoarse from crying. "I don't ever want to say his name again. Not now. Not ever."

They got to their feet, cold and emotionally drained. Hand in hand they walked back past the tree and as they did so, Maggie's hand brushed against the trunk. She barely noticed the tingle course up her arm.

When it was time for Phil to leave on Sunday afternoon, neither of them wanted to part. He had been kind and gentle all weekend and Maggie had basked in a love and tenderness she hadn't known since the loss of her mother as a little girl.

He gave her a final kiss. "Don't ever doubt how much I love you. And never doubt how special you are."

She wrapped her arms around him. "Can't you stay – stay for ever?"

The cold wind ruffled her hair and he pushed the strands back with gentle fingers. "Maybe that's something we should think about."

He drove away and Maggie fed the chickens and shut them in. It was still light but she couldn't risk the fox. Three more brown eggs were awaiting collection and she smiled as she remembered Jack's words.

"You really are good layers, aren't you?" she said out loud to the six chickens all sitting in a row on their perch in the shed. They clucked back in sleepy response.

Maggie wandered back to the cottage, humming to herself. She felt light, as though her feet could leave the ground and she could fly if she wanted to. It was as though a great weight had lifted from her. One of her biggest fears had been extinguished. Once inside, she sat on the bed, hugging the sheets to her. She had told him and he still loved her. With tears of joy still misting her eyes she gazed out of the window into the garden. It was still light, the setting sun casting its last rays along the ground. Suddenly the air in the room became thick and heavy as though it were pressing on her. And then he was there. The man stood by the leaning yew tree, a brown and white collie lying at his feet. Maggie let out an audible gasp and gripped the sheets, her knuckles turning white. She didn't blink. He was the same as before; tired and sad. He was staring directly at her and the dog was looking up at him. Now she could see clearly the detail in his tweed jacket, browns and greens woven together. His trousers were tucked into heavy knee-high boots and he held a long walking stick in his right hand. Maggie held her breath until she had to gasp for air, blinking at the same time. He was still there. For a moment she was utterly convinced he had to be a real flesh and blood person. Then, without warning, he moved, striding out towards the cottage. The dog jumped to its feet and followed him. He moved swiftly towards the window from which Maggie was staring and her fear was gone. All she felt was the joy at seeing him. He reached the window and put his left hand out as though to something that was no longer there. In an instant he was inside the room. Without breaking stride he walked to the bed where Maggie sat, and as she reached out her arms to greet him, he vanished into the air just inches from her. She was vaguely aware of the dog, following behind, disappearing at her feet.

Terror and shock clattered down upon Maggie like a landslide. She didn't know how long she sat, clinging to the sheets, unable to move. Eventually she managed to call Rupert who trotted in happily from the kitchen. With trembling hands she grabbed the dog and pulled him to her.

"I don't think I can stay here," she said.

20

A Visit From the Past

"HAVE YOU GOT IT straight?" Geraldine said, thrusting a thick hardback samples book at Maggie.

It was Monday morning and Maggie hadn't slept. Her thoughts had been consumed by the experience in Keeper's Cottage; the vision of the man coming through the window played over and over in her mind.

She nodded vaguely. "I think so."

"You either know or you don't," Geraldine said. "Take these samples to Mrs Handley and tell her I've been called away. We were meeting a supplier, but I can't make it. These are fabric designs for the new restaurant chairs for her to choose from. I'm sure she can do that without me."

"What shall I tell her if she asks where you are?" Maggie asked, bracing for the response.

"Anything – one of the children is ill, that'll do. Do you think you can manage that?"

"Yes," Maggie said.

An hour later and Maggie was standing in Christina Handley's drawing room. A fair-haired man in a suit sat at the table spreading out fabric samples. Maggie thought he looked young to be a rep and he seemed nervous. His smooth, boy-like face made his suit appear more like a school uniform. Maggie was annoyed at herself as she felt her own confidence rise in the presence of his timidity.

"Where is Geraldine?"

It was the inevitable question.

"I'm sorry, Mrs Handley, she can't make it; I think one of her children is ill."

Christina's blue eyes lingered on Maggie for a second longer than expected. *She is trying to read if I'm lying,* Maggie thought. A heated flush rushed across her face.

Maggie passed over the file. "She asked me to give you these."

"I wanted Geraldine's opinion on them. I'd hoped to make the decision today and place the order. We have settled on the chair design but not the fabric," Christina said quietly, her gentle voice not disguising her disappointment. "Did she at least say which designs she preferred?"

"No. She didn't say anything other than to give the book to you for you to decide."

Maggie detected a darkening in Christina's pale face, and then she smiled at the young man.

"Well, Mr Taylor, I'm afraid our manager has been detained. It looks like it's down to the three of us. Pull up a chair, Maggie, and let's get started."

"Mrs Handley, I'm sure you don't need me. And anyway, Geraldine prefers that I don't get involved with this kind of thing." The words tumbled out.

"Geraldine isn't here and I would like another opinion." Christina beckoned Maggie to the table. "And anyway, I'm interested to know what you think."

They sat together and chose their favourite designs while the company rep produced a steady supply of fabric samples. Despite the worry caused by her involvement in Charlotte's paintings, Maggie had gained confidence in her own opinion and soon found that she was offering suggestions uninvited. Even the young Mr Taylor seemed to grow in both stature and years as he relaxed in the genteel company of the two ladies. Many samples were dismissed without a thought and others came back around for a second and third look. The country-house style of fabrics from Greeff and Laura Ashley were the favourites and after two hours they had settled on three from which to make the final decision. Maggie's eye was constantly drawn to a floral and leaf design in pinks and greens with exotic pale blue birds settling here and there on random branches. Christina and Maggie laughed as they settled for the same design.

Mr Taylor left, happily clutching a substantial order for the new restaurant furniture plus additional pieces to be sold in the garden centre. After he had gone, Christina asked Maggie to stay. Maggie was still buzzing with enjoyment.

"Mrs Handley, I was thinking – why don't you have some of the designs from fabrics here in the manor reproduced? I think people would love to buy designs that come from here and that they don't see in other shops." She pointed to the fabric on the large sofa near the fire. "Like that – I didn't see anything like that design in all those samples – wouldn't it be exciting to produce our own…?" Maggie's voice trailed off as she saw Christina Handley smiling at her.

"Tell me, Maggie, how are you enjoying your role here?"

"Oh, I love it, thank you, Mrs Handley."

"What, all of it? There must be some mundane bits in administration. I hope you aren't getting bored."

Maggie felt the familiar surge of panic. Was she trying to trap her?

"No… I really do enjoy everything. And, even though I'm not involved in the buying, I like seeing new products come in and watching what sells."

Christina smiled. "Well, it seems to me that you are becoming involved in the buying. And what about the future? Do you have any long-term plans? Would you like to progress or are you happy as you are?"

Maggie blushed. "Oh, I'm more than happy as I am. The job is great and it's wonderful just being a part of this place." She hesitated, unsure what the purpose of the conversation was or where it was leading. "I have started studying, though. You know, to try and improve myself… but I haven't told anyone about that, especially Geraldine – I'm not sure what she would make of it."

"I think that's wonderful – and don't worry, I won't say a word to Geraldine." Christina observed Maggie for a few moments, a glimmer of sadness, or perhaps pity, crossing her face. "Geraldine is an incredible businesswoman, you know. I'm not sure what I would have done without her after Richard and I came here."

"Yes, she's very experienced," Maggie said, her heart sinking.

"But a bit frightening – don't you think?" A mischievous twinkle played in Christina's eyes.

Maggie couldn't work out if Christina was testing her loyalty or trying to find out how she really felt.

Maggie tried to sound light-hearted. "Yes, she can be, a little."

"Well, whatever happens don't lose sight of your own potential and thank you for your help today, Maggie, I really do appreciate it. As for your reproduction ideas – I'm going to give that some thought."

That was the signal for Maggie to leave and she walked to the door.

"Good luck with your studies," Christina said, "and keep up your good work here."

Maggie glanced back to see Christina observing her.

"I think George was right about you," she said, almost as if to herself.

Maggie closed the door, blushing. Something had just happened between Maggie and Christina, but she didn't understand quite what.

That evening, Anne arrived with her overnight bag.

"Wouldn't it be great if he appeared again?" Anne said as she unpacked her things.

She hadn't hesitated at coming over to stay with Maggie for a couple of nights to support her friend and help calm her nerves.

"Thanks for coming, Anne, but no, I'd rather he didn't put in another appearance."

"I know it must be creepy, but he's not hurting you, is he?"

"No, he isn't, but it's so weird. And it's how I feel when I see him. First I feel stunned that he's there and then I'm pleased to see him – somehow comforted by him. I think I even put my arms out to him. Can you believe that?"

"So how come you're so scared?"

"The fear comes afterwards. Once he's gone the shock of what happened hits me. Then I'm scared it will happen again."

"You really ought to tell Phil, you know," Anne said.

"I know, and I will, but not just yet."

Phil was already burdened with the news she'd broken to him over the weekend. She dare not ask him to understand something else about her – something she couldn't comprehend herself.

"Well, whatever happens, Maggie, you cannot give this place up. You love it too much."

"I don't want to leave. Perhaps I have to get used to sharing the place with him – I'm just not sure I can."

They were standing together in the bedroom and Maggie described the experience again.

"He was standing out there by the yew tree and I expected that I would blink and he'd disappear, like before, but he didn't." She pointed to the right of the two windows. "The next thing, he's walking quickly to the wall with the dog following. He reached out his hand and then… he was right here, in the room. That's when I felt strangely happy to see him – but why would I feel like that and then be so terrified afterwards?"

Anne ignored the question. "Didn't you say that was where the old back door used to be? Don't you think he was entering the cottage as he'd always done; reaching out to open a door that is no longer there?"

Maggie closed her eyes and tried to remember the experience in detail. "I think you're right. I saw him reach out and then – yes – for a split second I could see the garden behind him, as though through an open door."

"There you go. I think he is just going about his business as he always did; he isn't even aware of you."

"You might be right, but I'm telling you, Anne, he looks right at me as though he can see me. I'm not sure my nerves can stand not knowing when and where he might appear next. I managed a few minutes' sleep last night and that's all."

"The first thing you do is get some rest," Anne said, unpacking her bag onto the bed. "I'll stay in here and you sleep on the sofa – just for a couple of nights. Then we'll decide what to do."

Maggie was comforted knowing that her friend was in the next room, but sleep did not come easily. The clock ticked on past midnight and she wondered if Anne was asleep. At three o'clock she was jolted awake by the sound of tinkling metal. She sat up, straining to hear. The sound stopped. Maggie crept from the sofa to the hallway. Rupert lay in his basket in the kitchen, lazily scratching and catching his metal name tag with his claws. As he did so, it rattled against his collar. Maggie let out a long breath and stroked his head. The door to the bedroom swung open and Maggie jumped.

"If you could see your face," Anne said, heading to the sink for a glass of water. "What are you doing up?"

"I thought I heard something – it was just Rupert. Are getting some sleep?"

"Like a baby – your bed is so comfortable. That plus no snoring from Tom – I'm in heaven. See you in the morning."

Anne stayed for another night and Maggie slept soundly. To Maggie's relief and Anne's disappointment, nothing was seen or heard of the man.

Maggie, now feeling refreshed and her nerves a little settled, reassured Anne she would be fine on her own. By the time Phil arrived on Friday evening, her courage had returned. She hoped that the wandering spirit of Joseph Wells would leave her alone, but if it didn't, she tried to convince herself that it could do her no harm.

That Saturday, the fifth of December, and a week since Maggie had told him about her past, Phil suggested they walk to what was now a favourite place for both of them. The first snow of winter had fallen overnight; only two or three inches, but enough to blanket the parkland in white. They wandered together through a pristine wonderland, marked only by the tracks of deer and sheep, and here and there the broad prints of a badger. As they walked, Maggie detected a tension in Phil she hadn't seen in him before. He was subdued and his efforts at joviality were forced. Apprehension swept through Maggie. Something was wrong. He avoided every effort she made to get him to talk and diverted her attention by throwing snowballs for the dogs and at Maggie. By the time they arrived at the oak tree, they were as exhausted from running and strained laughter, as they were from the steep climb.

From above, the white park looked flat and featureless. The dead reeds of the marsh showed as a grey-yellow mass, and the river was like a ribbon of lead.

Phil gazed across the landscape and Maggie noticed that his face looked drawn and his eyes tired.

"Are you okay?" Maggie asked, hooking her arm into his.

He was silent for a moment and then pulled her close to him. "After what you told me last week, I wanted us to come back here to talk."

Maggie's heart pounded, *oh God, he's had time for it to sink in — he's changed his mind.*

"I wanted to ask you a question, but first I have to tell you something — something I was never going to reveal to anyone, but…" He turned his head away so Maggie couldn't see his face.

Her voice shook as she spoke. "Go on."

"After what you told me — I had to let you know." He kept his head turned away. "I have a child."

Maggie let go of his arm and her hand fell away. "What do you mean? Why didn't you tell me?"

"Because no one knows, not even my family – especially my family."

Maggie walked away to the oak tree and leaned against it as she gathered her thoughts. She watched him standing on the rocky edge, his back to her. *I told you everything and yet I know so little about you.*

After a while he came and joined her.

"You scared me," Maggie said. "I thought you were going to say you didn't want me."

"Never," Phil said, "but now I'm worried what you will think of me."

"Can you tell me about it?" Maggie asked, searching the brown eyes that she had never seen troubled until today.

"It was two years ago. She was a girl I'd known for a few months. I suppose it was serious enough, but we'd never made any plans. Then one day she left. She said she didn't love me; that she couldn't see it working for us."

Maggie could see the sadness in his face and felt a surge of pity. "I'm sorry, Phil, you must have been heartbroken."

His brow crinkled into a frown and he shook his head. "No, Maggs, that's the point, I wasn't sad at all. To tell the truth I was relieved. I knew we weren't right together." He gazed down at the ground, pushing the snow with his foot. "But then I heard she was pregnant. I went to see her – asked if the baby was mine. She said he was."

"He?"

Phil nodded without looking at her.

"Are you sure he is yours?"

"As sure as I can be. She said she'd left because she didn't want to be part of a relationship I was forced into. She wanted to keep the baby, but she didn't want anything from me."

They stood in silence as droplets of water fell around them from the branches above making tiny craters in the snow. The dogs had given up waiting for snowballs to be thrown and now snuffled about in the slush following animal tracks into the wood.

Maggie had a million questions she wanted ask; *what is the woman's name? Where does she live? What's the baby's name?* She asked none of them. "What did you do?"

Phil raised his head. "That's what I feel so bad about. I did nothing. I was just relieved. I don't know if she's managing okay. I paid her what I had in savings and that was it. She let me go and I ran for the hills. I've opened a bank account for him – you know, to perhaps help him in the future – but that's all. Then you told me about what happened to you and I felt so bloody selfish. I've always felt guilty, but now I feel ashamed."

Maggie took his hand and squeezed it. "You didn't do 'nothing'. You did what you could and you still are. It was her choice. Looks like we both had secrets, but let's make sure there aren't any more." Even as she said the words, she knew there was something she was keeping from him.

"I was scared you would think so badly of me. I mean it, Maggie, if she had needed me I would have been there for her, but she said she didn't."

"I think she will know you well enough to get in touch if she does need help – don't you think?" She thought for a moment and taking a deep breath added, "But, it wouldn't hurt for you to contact her and just remind her of that, would it?"

Phil pulled her to him. "You are so special, Maggie, I don't think you have a clue how much."

They walked back to Keeper's Cottage through the melting snow in silence; each immersed in their own thoughts. Despite the surprise of Phil's confession, she felt closer to him. He had revealed his closest kept secret to her and she loved him all the more for it. They had both made mistakes in their lives.

Once inside the cottage, they huddled by the warm fire.

"What was the question you were going to ask me?" Maggie said, only now remembering the comment Phil had made in the wood.

"I wasn't sure if it was appropriate, especially after what I've told you – but here goes." He pulled himself off the sofa and got onto his knees. Bracken ran over to him, tail wagging in anticipation of a game and Phil pushed her away. Her response was to bounce back and jump up trying to lick his face.

"Get lost, Bracken, this is serious." He turned on his knees to face Maggie who was trying hard to subdue a fit of giggles. "I know this is quick and we've only known each for a few months, but I want you to know how much I love you and what you mean to me. Today has made me realise that more." His dark eyes were so earnest that she was convinced a 'but' was about to follow.

He produced a small box from his pocket and opened it. A delicate gold ring with a single small diamond lay on a velvet cushion.

"Will you marry me?"

Maggie's hands shot to her mouth to quell a shriek of surprise, then reaching down and pulling his head to her, she leaned down and kissed him.

"Yes," she said.

Phil went to his car and returned with a bottle of champagne.

"I thought I'd bring this on the off chance you said 'yes'."

"You won't believe this, but I've never had champagne before."

"Well, I can't think of a better time to start," he said, popping the cork.

They spent the remainder of the day snuggled up in the warmth of the cottage and made their plans. They decided there was no rush; after all, Maggie hadn't even met Phil's family yet.

"I'll take you to meet the folks next weekend – what do you think?" Phil said, stretching his feet out in front of the fire and burying them beneath the sleeping Rupert.

"That makes me nervous," Maggie said. "What if they don't like me?"

"Who could not like you?" Phil said, ruffling her hair.

The weather turned mild overnight and by Sunday the snow that had briefly turned the park into a sparkling wonderland was almost gone. Phil disappeared into the enclosure where the chickens were now housed, to continue cutting back the overgrown bushes and trees, while Maggie tidied up around the outside of the cottage.

She smiled as she swept the last of the slush from the paths. It was a smile she was convinced had not left her face since Phil's proposal – even in her sleep. It was all so unreal. She had known him for only a matter of weeks, but in her heart it felt so right, so wonderful. She swept the brush again, the bristles flicking the wet snow into her face. Her smile erupted into laughter.

The voice seemed to come from nowhere.

"So, this is where you ended up?"

Maggie's blood turned to ice in her veins and her breath caught. She looked up to find Adam staring at her. She froze. So it was him she'd seen after all. She had persuaded herself that she had been mistaken, but now here he was, standing just feet away on the other side of the garden railings.

She hadn't seen him in eight months and he hadn't changed. He stood, cocky and confident, in his designer jeans and sheepskin bomber jacket. His skin was smooth and tanned and his dark hair swept back. His arm was draped around a pretty young woman who stood by his side.

"This is the one I told you about," he said. His voice was low and controlled but his eyes were locked on Maggie.

The woman was tall and slender, her long black hair shining in the weak sunlight. She smiled and nodded a silent 'hello' and leaned in closer to Adam.

"So, Maggie, what are you up to? Doing a few odd jobs for someone, are you?" He was trying to sound relaxed but

Maggie knew his voice well, she could detect the tension in it.

"I live here." Maggie's voice was a dry croak.

Adam looked around the park. "Found yourself a decent spot. How did you swing that one?"

Any words or thoughts evaporated in Maggie's head. Fear, shock and embarrassment all combined to render her mute. Her distress was clear and she could see Adam secretly revelling in it.

"See what I mean about her," Adam whispered to his companion. "Come on, Maggie – we're only interested in what you've been doing."

"Leave it, Adam," the woman said, "you're embarrassing her."

"Don't worry, Rebecca – she's like this all the time. How I stayed with her so long I'll never know."

Maggie wanted nothing more than for the ground to open up and remove her from this nightmare. And yet even as she took in his words, all an act for his girlfriend, she was aware of the faintest glimmer of something in his eyes – something she hadn't seen before that he was fighting to hide behind the bravado. It was regret.

Maggie's legs grew weak, and for one awful moment she thought she might faint. At that instant arms enveloped her from behind. Phil had rounded the corner of the cottage where he must have listened, unseen. She slumped back against him.

"Hi, you must be Adam. I'm Phil. What brings you to our neck of the woods?" His voice was calm and strong, and to

Maggie he sounded more confident than Adam. Just hearing his voice and feeling his body renewed her strength.

It was Adam who now stumbled over his words.

"Oh, it was err… Rebecca who knew about this place," he nodded towards the woman, "and she pestered me to bring her."

You're a liar. You found out I was here and you were looking for me, Maggie thought.

"Excuse me!" Rebecca said, as though reading Maggie's thoughts. "It was you who wanted to come here."

Phil ignored the woman. "Maggie has told me so much about you," he continued in the same unruffled tone. "It's great to get a chance to thank you."

Adam's face had darkened beneath his tan. *He didn't expect to see me with a man,* Maggie thought as she watched his discomfort grow.

The swagger in his voice sounded forced. "Oh, yes. Thank me for what?"

"For allowing this kind, intelligent and beautiful woman to slip through your fingers. If it wasn't for you, I wouldn't be the one lucky enough to be marrying her next summer and living with her in this amazing place." Phil's arms squeezed Maggie tighter.

"Well, good luck with her – that's all I can say." Adam started to back away from the railings. He was no longer enjoying the conversation.

"We don't need luck, Adam. It's something called love – a concept I doubt you'll ever experience." Phil's voice was light and Maggie could tell he was smiling as he spoke.

Maggie could see Adam's face changing. His jaw tightened and his lips pressed together in a thin line as he clenched his teeth; it was an expression she had seen many times before. He sensed he was being mocked and was fighting to keep control in front of his girlfriend. He was losing the battle. The words spat out in a vehement tirade.

"That's not something I'd ever want to experience with a worthless whore of a bitch like that." He pointed at Maggie.

It was as though Maggie watched from outside her body, as two things happened simultaneously. The woman, Rebecca, pushed herself away from Adam, staring at him in disgust. At the same moment, Phil let go of Maggie and placing one hand on the railings vaulted over them. It took him a second to reach Adam and grabbing him by his coat, punched him square in the face. Adam's nose exploded in a gush of blood and he staggered backwards, falling to the ground.

Maggie watched dumbfounded as Phil dragged Adam to his feet. He was five inches shorter than Adam and yet appeared infinitely stronger. It was as though Adam was shrinking before her eyes as he held up his hands defensively and tried to scramble away. She could picture herself doing the same thing as she'd tried to save her baby.

Phil held on and yanked Adam back towards him. "If you ever set foot near this place again, or come within a mile of Maggie, you will regret it. Now get out of my sight," he said, pushing Adam away. With blood still pouring from his broken nose Adam fell back to the ground.

"Rebecca – I think that's your name," Phil said, turning to the woman. "This man batters women and he kills unborn babies. If he hasn't hurt you yet – he will. He should be in prison and if he ever comes here again – that's where he'll end up. Now get his sorry arse away from my fiancé's home."

Rebecca turned and walked away leaving Adam on the ground. "He can find his own way back," she called over her shoulder.

Adam got to his feet and holding his hands to his battered face, he broke into a staggering run after her.

Phil returned to the garden, this time via the gate. He put his hands gently on Maggie's shoulders and looked into her pale face. "There you go, Maggs," he said. "That's one more thing you don't have to worry about."

Maggie folded herself into the safety of his arms. Her body was still shaking and her heart pounding. He held her tightly until she could speak.

"You were brilliant," she whispered.

"I know – I have many talents, some of which you are yet to see."

She kissed him and hugged him. "I love you so much. What did I do to deserve you?"

"You didn't have to do anything. You were just you."

21

Mary

DURING MONDAY'S LUNCH BREAK, Maggie went home and was surprised to find a letter on the doormat revealing that John Charlton had already replied to her. After letting the dog into the garden and making herself a coffee, she settled in the living room to read the letter. He thanked Maggie for contacting him and said he was delighted that she was enjoying life at Keeper's Cottage. He said that his research had brought him into contact with several distant relatives who had supplied him with more information. He enclosed a newspaper clipping and a photograph he thought would be of particular interest to her. Maggie looked into the envelope and took out the copy of a black and white photograph. Joseph Wells, now beyond all doubt the man she had seen, stared back at her from across time.

The photograph showed him standing with his family in the garden at Keeper's Cottage. The garden was unrecognisable but for the railings around the perimeter, which were visible in the background, and in the centre of the picture stood Joseph. He looked just as she'd seen him, though he appeared to have smartened himself for the photograph. He was clean-shaven and his long hair combed back. He was wearing a tweed jacket and trousers that were tucked into long boots. At his side sat a dog – the dog she had also seen with him. Also in the picture were two children. A sturdy young man of perhaps fifteen stood to Joseph's left and in front of them a little girl of perhaps four years of age.

The original photograph had writing in faded pencil on the back and that, too, had been copied. It read; *Joseph, Jack and Mary, and Paddy the dog. January 1871.*

"Mary"! Maggie whispered the name out loud.

With trembling fingers, she unfolded the copy of a newspaper cutting. It was from the *Ashford Times* dated 26th May 1871, and read:

Tragedy strikes at Langley

The head forester at Langley Manor, Joseph Wells, committed suicide on 20th May 1871. He had been ill following the death of his wife early last year and the death of his daughter, Mary, to tuberculosis in April this year. His surviving son, Jack, returned from work to discover his father's body and that of his dog in Langley Park, not far from Keeper's Cottage where he lived. It is believed he turned his shotgun on himself after first shooting his dog. Owner of Langley, Philip Handley, said the whole estate was saddened at the loss of a dedicated and trusted worker and friend. Joseph Wells was 43 years old.

Maggie gazed at the photograph again. The little girl stood in front of her father. Her dark hair was tied up in a ribbon and she was wearing what might have been her best coat, a scarf tucked snugly around her neck. Now, as Maggie looked again, she could see that the little girl was thin and tired. Within a few weeks of this photograph being taken she would be dead – and so would her father. Maggie gazed around the room – *their room* – and she felt tears sting her eyes. It had all become so clear. Now she understood Joseph's pain, why he was returning to the cottage, calling and whispering to his daughter in the weeks before she died. The fear lifted from her. All that was left was sadness.

That evening Anne arrived and embraced Maggie in an affectionate hug.

"I'm so pleased for you, Maggie, and for Phil. You are going to have a wonderful life together, I just know it."

They opened a bottle of wine and Maggie poured two glasses. She passed a glass to her friend. "I've got some amazing information about the cottage – I received a letter at lunchtime from Joseph Wells' ancestor." She hesitated and took a sip of wine. "But first I want to tell you about someone else. I want to tell you about Adam."

"Who's Adam?"

The dramatic events of the day before had released the memories that had been locked inside her for so long. She had revealed what Adam had done to her to Phil and it was the best thing she could have done. Now, after seeing Adam so humiliated, he had suddenly become insignificant. Witnessing his weakness had made her feel stronger and she knew that telling Anne about him would purge any lingering hold he had.

Anne was shaken. "I realised you must have had a tough time from how you behaved and the things you said — or almost said. But, Maggie, I never imagined how bad it was. I'm so sorry." She put her arm around Maggie's shoulders. "But you know he should never be allowed to get away with what he did to you. If you want Tom to help, he would be more than happy to advise and support you."

Even after reliving once more the details of her past, Maggie felt calm and content.

"Thank you, Anne, but no. I don't want to fight with him. It won't change anything. Yes, he has done things that will affect me for the rest of my life — but I'm lucky. I escaped. I ended up here and I met Phil. It's time for me to move on." She smiled at her friend. "I think I've discovered how to be happy."

"You are incredibly wise, Maggie, and brave. Just remember, if you change your mind, you know where we are. Now, tell me again — did Phil hit the bastard really hard. Do you think he broke his nose?"

Maggie laughed. "Yes, Anne. I think he really did." She put her hand on her friend's and squeezed it. "Thank you for listening. Now I think this is the last time I will ever say the name 'Adam'."

Anne put the newspaper clipping down and took a long swig from her glass.

"Now that's a sad story," she said.

"Isn't it?" said Maggie. "Not only have we found out who he was, we know that he took his own life and why he did it;

the poor man. And I now know who Mary was and why I've heard him calling to her."

"It's horrible to think of him somehow trapped, searching for his dead daughter."

"It's a dreadful thought," Maggie said. "But one thing I know is that I'm not scared any more. If I see him again, I'll tell him I know who he is. I'll tell him I know what happened to him and that I'm happy to share this place with him."

"Perhaps he's one more ghost you've laid to rest?" said Anne.

Rupert came over and rested his head on Maggie's knee and she gazed around the cottage, smiling. "Perhaps he is."

———

The diamond solitaire flashed in the winter sunlight. Maggie couldn't stop looking at it as though at any moment it might vanish from her hand.

"Don't expect to get another one for Christmas," Phil said, grinning from ear to ear.

They had just left his parents' farm where his mother had made a huge fuss of Maggie.

"I told you she'd love you. I never doubted it for a second. It's me she's annoyed with for not introducing you sooner."

"They are so warm-hearted. Now I know where you get it from," Maggie said. "Do you know how lucky you are to have a family like that?"

"Well, if I'm lucky, what does that make you? They belong to you as much as me and you've not had to put years of training into them."

Maggie gave him a playful slap.

"You are cheeky," she said, and then frowned. "It won't be like this when you meet my father, you know."

"Don't worry about that. You know how lovable I am."

Maggie didn't laugh. She doubted her father had ever loved anyone, not even her mother.

Phil tried to reassure her. "Listen, Maggie, it doesn't matter. We will let him know because it's the right thing to do. It's up to him then. We won't allow him to spoil anything. He can be involved or not, but we don't need him to be."

Maggie felt her spirits lift. "No, we don't."

Langley Manor closed to the public on the last weekend before Christmas. The great hall was bedecked with a twenty-foot Christmas tree and a huge log fire was lit each day. Maggie watched as the light from the flames reflected on a hundred baubles; she thought it a shame that only the family and staff got to see such an impressive sight. For a few moments, it was as though she was a child, pretending she was a local peasant girl allowed into the grand house at Christmas to take a privileged peek. She smiled at the thought and then closed the oak doors on the festive scene and headed to the garden centre.

A final count was to take place while stock was at its lowest levels and before the January and February deliveries for the new season. Today all hands were on deck to get the job done in one go.

Maggie kept a note of the items that had been altered on the previous count and positioned herself to make sure she would count at least some of the same items. When she came to the pretty garden chairs and tables, she double and triple-checked the numbers. Geraldine did not count herself but moved among the staff checking that all areas were covered. When Maggie had the opportunity, she slipped away to the stockroom to make certain there were no more chairs and tables. There were none. This time she knew beyond any doubt that her quantities were correct.

The following morning, Maggie called at the security room in the gatehouse.

"Morning, Charlie, there didn't happen to be a late delivery last night by any chance?" Maggie asked in as 'matter-of-fact' way as she could muster.

"I wasn't on, love, I'll just check."

Maggie waited. It suddenly seemed ridiculous to suspect Geraldine in this way, and she became evermore certain the answer from Charlie would be 'no'.

He opened the logbook, taking an age to find the right page. "Aye, there was. Geraldine Walker saw them in again." He looked up at Maggie, grinning. "She must like what they sell to put up with their dilatory ways."

Maggie felt her heart thumping. "She certainly must, Charlie. Thanks very much."

The last working day before the holiday break arrived and for two days Maggie had not laid eyes on the stock sheets. She checked with Anne if they'd gone to the accounts department, but Anne hadn't seen them either. Nor had Geraldine approached Maggie regarding any alterations. *Perhaps she daren't try it twice,* Maggie thought.

Maggie wore her engagement ring for the first time at work and it didn't take long for Pam to spot it. She was holding Maggie's hand to take a closer look when Geraldine entered the office.

"Maggie has some news," Pam said, eager to get in first.

Geraldine came over and examined the ring. "Congratulations, Maggie," she said. "I'm pleased for you." Her face softened and a glimmer of a smile touched her lips. She appeared to be genuinely pleased.

"Thank you," Maggie said, responding to the hint of warmth. "We are both so happy."

"I suppose the next thing is you'll be pregnant and wanting time off?" It was as though Geraldine had realised she'd let her guard down for an instant and struck back quickly.

Maggie felt heat come to her face, but this time it wasn't embarrassment, it was anger. "We don't have any plans for getting married yet, so we certainly don't have plans for a family," she said, fighting to keep her voice level. She had never spoken like that to Geraldine before.

Geraldine appeared to note the new firmness in Maggie's voice and responded. "Good, I pay you to work, not to be off having babies." She walked away towards her office door.

Maggie watched her go, her blood simmering. She spoke before she could stop herself.

"Do you have the paperwork for last night's delivery?"

Geraldine stopped in her tracks and turned to face Maggie. Her green eyes flashed and for a second she didn't speak, as though composing herself.

"You are mistaken; there was no delivery last night."

Maggie held her gaze longer than she had ever done before and she knew that the intended threat had registered.

22

Trapped in the Roots

MAGGIE HAD NEVER LOOKED forward to Christmas more than this year. She and Phil had ten days off work and they planned to spend every moment of that time together. They had been invited to spend Christmas Day with Phil's family and Boxing Day with Anne and Tom. Her only concern was her father. She had held off speaking to him for too long and as time had passed, the harder it became. On Christmas Eve she telephoned him.

"Hello, Dad, it's me, I wanted to wish you a happy Christmas."

"Oh, thought I might hear from you eventually."

You have my number, you could have called me, Maggie thought, fighting the anxiety that clutched at her.

"Did you get my card? I sent it last week."

"Yes, I think it's somewhere." There was silence for a long moment before he spoke again. "What do you want?"

I'm your daughter; it's Christmas; I wanted to speak to you, to let you know how happy I am; to tell you about Phil. She remembered Phil's words 'it's up to him, we don't need him', and she felt her strength grow. When she spoke it was in a calm and detached voice.

"I also wanted to let you know that I'm getting married next year." Silence followed. "He's a wonderful man called Phil. I will let you know the details when they're fixed."

"So, you've shacked up with someone else, have you?"

"Dad, why are you like this? What did I do other than leave you and live with a man out of wedlock? Is that the only reason you despise me so – or is it that I remind you of Mum?"

There was no response. Maggie remained composed. This time there was no tremble in her voice; no tightening in her throat. She had something to say and she would say it.

"Do I remind you of how you treated her? Did you think I was too young to know? You succeeded in driving me out only to find the same existence that Mum had with you. But I saved myself. I've found a happiness she never did. Don't take your guilt out on me."

Maggie expected to hear the receiver slam down, but it didn't. She took a deep breath.

"We would like you to come to the wedding and we would like you to visit us. Despite everything, we want you to be part of our lives." She found the words easier to say than she expected. She felt at peace. This was what her mother would have wanted.

"We'll see," was the curt reply.

Maggie found herself smiling. "I hope you're okay, Dad. I'm truly happy and you can be a part of that, but it's entirely up to you. You know where I am. Happy Christmas," she said, and put the receiver down, knowing there would be no reply.

She looked up to see Phil standing in the doorway, the corners of his mouth tilting upwards, a look of pride shining in his eyes.

She shrugged her shoulders. "One less thing to worry about."

It was a time when Maggie finally felt like she belonged and she basked in the comfort and company of people who welcomed her as one of their own. Phil's family could not have made her feel more at home on Christmas Day. The farmhouse had been decorated throughout with garlands and holly, and dinner, prepared by Phil's mum and sisters-in-law for fifteen people, was spectacular. *So this is what being part of a family feels like,* Maggie thought as she beamed across the table at Phil. The following day was spent with Anne and her family, and the festivities were completed by a visit to Jack and Irene. Irene fussed over Maggie and Phil like a contented mother hen, feeding them until they couldn't move. It had been the happiest three days of Maggie's life, and now she wanted nothing more than to settle back home with Phil and the dogs.

The winter had been gentle so far, but four days after Christmas Day a ferocious storm hit the south of the country. The winds picked up during the evening and gained in strength overnight. Maggie lay awake in bed, as the roof creaked and the windows rattled in the building storm. An almighty gust brought an ear-splitting crack as a tree snapped before crashing to the ground out in the park. Maggie sat up in bed listening to the frightened whimpers of the dogs. The next blast shook the timbers of the cottage and Maggie grasped Phil's arm, convinced the roof would be lifted off. Phil jumped out of bed and led Maggie into the hallway, the centre of the building, and there they remained, huddled together with the dogs as the gale roared across the parkland, battering the exposed cottage.

Around five o'clock the next morning, the storm finally eased. It was still too dark to check the damage and Phil went to sleep, but Maggie lay awake, restless. The violence of the storm had brought back a vague memory she couldn't quite bring to mind and she tried to recall it as she drifted into a half sleep.

The dream crept gently upon her. She was walking along a narrow path towards her favourite place, but the way was barely visible, no more than a track made by wild animals. It was hard work and she felt breathless. Her chest hurt and her legs were stiff. All around were fallen trees and branches and she had to step carefully over the debris that lay across her path. Suddenly, she was there by the oak tree. It lay like a great beast, cut down, broken and dying. Its lower limbs had snapped off, the jagged edges driven deep into the soft ground. Its upper branches waved in the breeze as though it were making one last feeble effort to rise. She reached out and touched the bark, stroking the giant tree as though to comfort it. And then she cried as with grief at the loss of a long and trusted friend. Then, as can only happen in a dream, the first shoots of spring appeared and the woodland around her was touched by fresh green. She walked with aching legs to the rocky edge and came to a stone outcrop from which she could look out over the valley below. There she sat, as she had done many times before during her long life.

She remembered the squeals of laughter of her friends as they had played in the woods. She had climbed below the rocks, staying hidden for the longest time while the others had tried to find her, shouting and calling to her. She remembered sitting there for the first time with the man who would become her husband and how they had fallen in love with this place as they had fallen in love with each other. Now he was gone.

She looked down on the valley, farmed with crops and cattle and pigs for as far as the eye could see. Cottages scattered here and there, with a cluster of houses together in the village way off to the left, smoke rising from chimneys in the distance. Directly below, builders were at work on the landowners' new house. It would be grander than the one that had stood before it and she hoped the owner would continue to be kind to her family as they scraped a living from the land. To the right, she could see her own tiny thatched cottage, standing with five others. Men working hard among the ridge and furrow fields looked like specks. They were her sons. She was grieving, but as she watched her family, her heart swelled with pride.

Then she remembered what she carried in the pocket of her apron. She had seen the tiny oak sapling near the path and on impulse had bent stiffly to ease it from the soil. Now, with gnarled fingers, she lifted the sapling from her apron, careful not to damage the fragile roots. Moving away from the rocky edge she searched for a suitable place to plant it. Close to the fallen oak stood a large, peculiar boulder she had known all her life. It had always seemed out of place, sitting alone among the trees. On the side facing away from the cliff edge, the stone had split leaving a gaping crevice. Carefully she planted the oak into the cleft.

Then she was standing in silent prayer. The tree was a symbol of continuing life and she hoped it would grow strong for many hundreds of years to come. She rested her hand against the boulder; she felt old and tired. She doubted she could make the climb again, but she prayed that she might have the chance to return to this special place once more.

Maggie sat up with a start, breathing hard, her face wet with tears. She held up her hands. There was no sign of the gnarled red knuckles and her skin was soft and supple once more. The dream had been so real, every detail, every intense feeling etched into her memory.

Phil was sound asleep and she eased herself out of bed and tiptoed to the window. A grey light came through the curtain and she pulled it back.

The garden was strewn with branches and twigs. Here and there stone slates from the roof had sliced into the lawn, standing up like miniature gravestones. The leaning yew tree had lost its battle and lay forlorn on the ground.

She shivered and rubbed her arms as goosepimples rose on her skin. Joseph appeared before her eyes, standing near the yew close to the upturned roots, his dog at his side. He looked exactly as he had before. Without hesitation, Maggie raised her hand to wave to him and then held up the tiny carved horse for him to see. She hadn't been able to find it and she wanted it for something special. She felt a surge of joy as he smiled back at her in acknowledgement. Then he was gone.

Maggie stood dazed. Her hand was empty, and yet she could still sense the feel of the carved figure in her hand. Now, as she recovered herself, she felt no fear. She knew Joseph; she understood his grief. Even though he was no longer there, she spoke to him.

"I'm so sorry, Joseph," she whispered. "I'm sorry for you and your wife and your little daughter. But they aren't here anymore. Mary isn't here. Please be at peace."

"Did you say something?" Phil murmured, turning over in bed and stretching.

"I said the yew tree has blown down."

The damage was bad, but it could have been worse. The largest trees between the edge of the marsh and Keeper's Cottage had withstood the storm and miraculously, even the henhouse had survived, though its inhabitants were quiet and subdued after the terrors of the night. But out across the park, several oaks and beeches lay pitifully on the ground.

Phil returned from the manor with some plastic sheets to temporarily cover the holes in the roof left by the missing slates. He saw Maggie standing in the garden by the fallen yew.

"It was never going to hang on much longer, not the way it was leaning," he said joining her.

"I know," Maggie said, "but it's still sad."

"Better than the thing falling on us one day when we least expect it."

"I suppose so." Maggie peered into the large hole left by the upturned roots. She crouched down to look closer. The edge of a buried stone wall showed through the crumbling soil. "I wonder what this was."

Phil got on his hands and knees next to her and Maggie shuffled along to make room. As she did, something entangled in the upturned stump caught her eye. She pulled the soil away from an object firmly trapped in the roots along with a flat stone. The soil immediately beneath the tree trunk was surprisingly dry and as it crumbled away in Maggie's hands she realised what the object was. It was as though she had received an electric shock. She leapt to her feet, staggered backwards and fell to the floor. Everything went black.

Maggie came to a minute later resting against Phil. She was lying on the wet grass, trembling uncontrollably. She tried to speak, but the words stuck in her throat and only a hoarse whisper emerged. Phil told her not to talk and supported her back inside the cottage and onto the sofa. After a few sips of hot, sweet tea, the colour returned to Maggie's face.

"I'm going to call a doctor, just to make sure you're okay," Phil said, still concerned.

"I'm all right, I just stood up too quickly," Maggie said, forcing a reassuring smile. "Really – I'm fine, let's go back out into the fresh air."

They stared at the underside of the dislodged stump. A square box was clearly visible though still encased in its prison of roots.

"I wonder how long this has been here," Phil said peering closer. "For as long as this yew has been here and I'd guess that must be more than a hundred years."

Maggie's gaze remained fixed on the container. She knew how long it had been there. She knew what was inside it. A peculiar sensation came over her as she gazed at the box. It was as if seeing it had released long-forgotten memories. It reminded her of the dream that morning.

She moved closer to the upturned roots and traced the edges of the container with her fingers. Phil reached forward and grabbed the box, pulling at it hard until it came away along with the stone that had been placed on top. He held it up and peered at it closely. It was heavy. The wood had split and cracked, and in places pieces had fallen away revealing a lead lining. As Phil brushed the remaining soil from it, roughly carved ivy leaves were revealed, winding around the sides. The lid was firmly sealed and despite his best efforts he was unable to dislodge it. He put it down to one side and started to hack away at the remaining roots still holding onto the upturned trunk.

"I'll free this up and then borrow a chainsaw. At least when we get those chimneys opened up, we'll have a good supply of firewood next year," Phil said.

He's forgotten what I told him, Maggie thought. *He doesn't know.*

She picked up the container and walked away.

"I'll take it to the shed and see if I can open it," she said trying to keep her voice light. "I'll leave the heavy work to you."

"Okay, love." He looked up at her. "Are you sure you feel all right?"

She turned away to hide her drained face. "I'm fine — stop worrying."

Grabbing a pair of leather gardening gloves to give her grip, she tried the lid of the container. At first it refused to shift, and then, with a grating sound, gave way. Maggie was scared to look inside — it would reveal something she dared not believe. She closed her eyes and the items appeared in her mind as clear as the day they had been placed inside the box. The fine silver chain that had belonged to her mother, the pipe she had seen her father smoke so many times until it had broken, her brother's pocketknife, and her own gift — the most precious thing she had.

Maggie lifted the lid and let the contents fall onto the workbench, kicking up dust as they fell. The silver chain was tarnished and black. The pocketknife had rusted no further and the bone handle was clean and smooth. Maggie picked up the pipe; it was split. The smell of tobacco came back to her, strong and sweet and she could see her own small hands helping to pack the soft weed into the bowl of the pipe.

She picked up the tiny wooden horse and ran her fingers along the roughly cut mane to the pointed ears and down to where the leg had broken off. She had loved it once but had been happy to leave it as a gift to her mother.

"How could I not have known him?" she said out loud.

She put the items into her pocket and, leaving the empty container on the bench, walked casually back past Phil.

"Well, did you manage to open it?"

"Yes, nothing special, just an old chain, a little knife and a broken pipe. Probably got thrown out by someone years ago." Maggie didn't mention the toy horse.

"And there was me thinking we'd found buried treasure," Phil said, getting back to his work.

"We did," Maggie whispered to herself.

Maggie sat at the kitchen table staring at the photograph of Joseph Wells and his family in the garden at Keeper's Cottage. There was Joseph, his dog sitting by his side. To his left stood his son, Jack, and in front of them his little girl, Mary. To the left of the picture and almost out of frame was something she hadn't noticed before. It was a low stone wall and, barely visible, a small amount of shimmering water. It was a pond and by the edge stood a tiny tree.

The memories continued to invade Maggie's mind, as though she had awakened from the longest of sleeps and was now recalling every dream she'd ever had. Her mother had gone and each of them had wanted to put something of theirs inside the box. Her father had placed her necklace inside along with the broken pipe that had been a gift from her. It was her brother who had placed the small penknife into the box; it was old – the first one he'd had. Tears began to trickle down Maggie's face at the memory of loss and confusion.

"We wanted to leave something of ours in her favourite place in the garden. I think it was a way of saying goodbye." She spoke out loud and a rhythmic thump answered her. Rupert had followed her inside and now gazed up at her as his tail rapped against the table leg. She wiped the tears from her cheeks on the back of her sleeve and stroked the rough grey hair of the dog's back. "How could I have forgotten?" she said. She laid the wooden horse by the photograph and stared into the face of the sick child, Mary. And she knew she had lived here before.

23

The Truth Revealed

FOR THE NEXT HOUR, Maggie remained motionless, staring at the photograph. Phil stayed out in the garden tidying up the storm damage, and she was pleased. She needed time to think; to assimilate what had happened.

She thought back – reliving everything she'd experienced, beginning with that first, dreadful journey to Langley and her discovery of the oak. She had thought she was suffering a breakdown at first and then, when she had seen Joseph, she was convinced she must be seeing a ghost. But there had always been something else – something more. She had felt it. Now she understood. She had never seen a ghost; Joseph was not a wretched, wandering spirit looking for his lost daughter. She had been Mary. She was seeing what Mary had seen. She had been reliving Mary's memories.

Maggie sat back in her chair and looked out of the window across to Langley Wood. "I was meant to come back," she said, with only Rupert to hear. "I was meant to find this place."

She thought of the day she'd found Langley, when she'd sat by the roadside not caring if she lived or died. It was as though reaching those terrible depths of despair had freed her to be drawn to this place. She had been pulled to it like a magnet and without knowing she had been guided home.

Phil came in, his face crimson from physical effort, brown hair plastered to his face.

"One of the workmen has just come down from the manor to see if we needed any help. He's going to give me a hand with the plastic sheeting."

"That's great," Maggie said. She hadn't heard a vehicle come by at all; she had been deep in thought – lost in another time. Now, as she spoke, her voice sounded alien to her. "I feel much better now. I think I will go for a walk and take the dogs. I want to see if the oak is okay."

Phil surveyed her with serious eyes. "You look a better colour than you did, but don't go too far."

"I won't."

Maggie walked through the wood, clambering over fallen branches and skirting around uprooted trees. Although the wind had dropped, a brisk breeze still bent the higher limbs of the surviving trees, threatening to dislodge broken branches that had been trapped in their fall and now hung precariously above the ground. Confused squirrels ran about in the undergrowth, shaken from hibernation as their dreys were ripped from the branches.

Bracken yapped in delight as she chased after them, Rupert following behind.

It was as though Maggie had stepped back into her dream. She watched her feet tread the path to the oak just as she'd done in her sleep and with a sinking feeling she waited for the fallen giant to come into view. As she rounded the bend in the path, Maggie closed her eyes. She couldn't bear to see the tree as it had appeared in her dream.

She opened her eyes a fraction, viewing through trembling lashes. The tree stood in all its ancient splendour as though the storm had never been. Maggie felt a surge of relief rush over her as she hurried forward, resting against the trunk and then bending down to run her hands over the thick roots that arched over the broken boulder and into the ground.

It had been so tiny, so fragile when she planted it. But the boulder had been the ideal place, it had sheltered the sapling just as she'd hoped it would, and now it had grown strong – the oldest tree in the wood. It was such a special place to her and she had prayed that she would have the chance to return.

Maggie snapped upright and stepped back from the tree. Everything became clear like a blurred picture brought into startling focus. She had lived before, here at Langley – and not only once as Mary, but perhaps many times. And it seemed to her that this was where the cycle had begun. She had planted this tree and had been inextricably linked to it throughout its long life. Here a secret veil had been pulled aside to allow her glimpses of her past – as Mary and as the old, tired woman who had loved this place more than 600 years ago. How many more memories might return to her – how many more lives? Perhaps she hadn't been meant to find out; perhaps it had been her mental state that had allowed her to enter. However it had happened, at that moment Maggie felt a change come over her. She felt the blood pumping in her veins, her breathing becoming deep and slow, her mind clearing. She felt strong.

The holidays were over. It was the second day of January 1987 and even though there wasn't a great deal of work to do, Maggie had difficulty concentrating on what little there was. She hadn't seen Geraldine since that last uncomfortable exchange between them, and events meant that she had given her little thought since. Now she found her mind straying between Geraldine and Joseph Wells and little Mary.

She was shaken from her daydreaming by voices at the door and in walked Geraldine with Christina Handley close behind.

"Hello, Maggie. Happy New Year to you," Christina said. "I hope you had a lovely Christmas – and I understand congratulations are in order."

"Thank you, Mrs Handley. Yes, Phil and I were engaged before Christmas and we have had a wonderful time over the holidays."

"I'm delighted for you both, and I would so like to meet your fiancé some time."

"Happy new year, Maggie," Geraldine said in a perfunctory manner.

"Thank you. I hope you had a good break, Geraldine."

"Yes, it was fine," Geraldine said, heading into her office.

Christina followed and beckoned Maggie to go with them.

"I have some news of my own I'd like to share with you both," Christina said, and Maggie could see that she was glowing with excitement. "Richard and I are expecting our first child. It has taken rather a long time and we could not be happier."

Maggie felt a rush of exhilaration for Christina and was unable to stop herself. "Oh, I'm so delighted for you, Mrs Handley. When is the baby due?"

Geraldine glared at Maggie. "I don't think Christina needs an inquisition."

"Don't worry at all – I'm just so thrilled to be able to talk about it. We wanted to wait until the three months were up – you know, just in case. Anyway, all is well and we expect our new arrival in June," Christina said, her eyes sparkling as she spoke.

Maggie realised that she didn't feel envy or sadness at the news, simply the enjoyment of sharing in another's happiness. She took it as a sign that her life had moved forward.

Geraldine mumbled her own congratulations after which came a short, stilted silence

"Anyway, let's get back to work, shall we?" Christina said. "I was just telling Geraldine on the way up what a help you were to me, Maggie, with the designs for the restaurant furniture. I'm so excited to see what it will look like."

"Oh, it was nothing," Maggie said, trying to making light of it.

"It was certainly something to me. I like to get the views of others before I make a decision. And I think we did quite well. Oh, and I mentioned your idea of reproductions to Richard and to Geraldine – I think it's something we should look into." Christina had settled into the chair opposite Geraldine's desk, but Maggie remained standing close to the door.

Geraldine surveyed Maggie for a moment and then turned her attention back to Christina. "You may as well know – I have put the order for the furniture on hold. I think we need to discuss it."

Maggie felt her muscles tighten as she watched the colour rise in Christina's cheeks. Silence hung in the room broken only by the intrusive rattle of a hail shower against the window.

"Oh, and why is that?" Christina said, an unnatural edge to her voice.

Geraldine sat behind her desk and reached for her cigarettes. "I saw what you'd ordered and I think you've made a mistake. There are several other designs that would be more suitable. Remember, we want to sell this product as well as have it look pretty in the restaurant."

Maggie's gaze settled on the floral patterns of the carpet while she silently urged Christina to fight back.

"Thank you for your concern," Christina said, "but I would like you to reinstate the order."

Geraldine nodded towards Maggie. "Christina has thanked you for your *help*. You can go now." Maggie noted the subtle emphasis of the word.

"That's all right," Christina said. "I would like Maggie to stay if we are going to discuss this again; I value her opinion."

Geraldine raised her eyebrows and turned her mouth downwards, as if to say, *'if you want a witness, so be it'*.

"I'm afraid I won't reinstate the order, Christina, because I know it's a mistake. I am employed by Richard to make a profit for this place and I will not have the success of the business put at risk by your whimsy."

"So that is what you think of my input is it?" Christina's voice was quiet and controlled.

"I think the business is a hobby to you, Christina, and you do not have the experience or, if I might be so bold, the eye, to make this kind of decision. That is what I am employed for."

For a long moment Christina remained seated, staring at Geraldine. Then she rose from her chair. "I don't see the point in continuing this conversation at the moment. We will discuss it again later." She walked from the room with dignity and quietly closed the door. Maggie's heart sank and she turned to leave.

"Stay here, I want to talk to you," Geraldine said.

Maggie moved back into the room and waited, watching Geraldine take her time as she lit her cigarette and looked through the papers on her desk. It was a long two minutes before Geraldine spoke.

"I've always had a good relationship with Christina – that is until you came." She didn't look at Maggie as she spoke and continued to turn the papers over. "Why are you trying to cause trouble between us?"

Maggie waited for the expected hot flush to race across her face and for her throat to tighten. It didn't happen. All she felt was a cool detachment as though she was watching a drama unfold on television. When she spoke it was as if she was reciting long-practised lines.

"I'm not trying to cause trouble, Geraldine. I'm simply doing what I'm asked to do – no more than that."

"Yes, I have noticed how you like to come across that way. But you see, I know you for what you are – a dim girl who will never make much of herself and thinks the best way to get on in life is to get in with those who have made a success of themselves."

"I'm sorry you feel that way, but you're wrong." Maggie's voice was calm and low. "All I want is to do a good job – for you and for Langley."

"Well, you seem to have failed to reach those aspirations. I have never seen so many mistakes made by one of my employees. And now you are actively leading the owner down a route that is way out of her depth. I think it's time I let you go."

Maggie studied Geraldine for long moments. She didn't make any kind of conscious decision about what she was going to say, the words simply emerged.

"You show proof of the mistakes I've made and then we can discuss the missing stock."

Geraldine's lips tightened together and Maggie noticed the array of fine smoker's lines appear around them.

"Don't threaten me. Clear your desk and leave this building. You have no place here."

Maggie listened to the words Geraldine spat out and felt as though she were floating. She felt light and calm.

"No, Geraldine, I will not."

"I think you have forgotten your place – I decide who stays and goes. Now get out." As she put the cigarette to her lips, her fingers trembled ever so slightly, the quiver travelling to the gold bracelet, which to Maggie's eyes now appeared dull and tarnished. Geraldine seemed to be aware that she was showing weakness and quickly played her ace card. "Oh, and you'd better start packing – you will be out of that cottage by the end of the month."

The hail returned with a flurry, rattling at the window like a snooping observer trying to get in, and the roof beams creaked and groaned in the wind as though the old house was joining the argument.

"I don't think that will be the case," Maggie said. "I hope to be at Langley and live in Keeper's Cottage for many years to come."

Geraldine stared at her, aghast; anger turning to rage.

"Who do you think you are speaking to? I said get out!"

Geraldine's fury made no impression on Maggie; the threats breaking like flimsy arrows against a wall. She stayed where she was, not taking her eyes off Geraldine and watching as red blotches appeared on her face and neck, the colour clashing with her copper hair.

"I know you are not a particularly bright girl, but I would have thought you could understand an instruction as simple as that." Geraldine pointed to the door and then, finally relinquishing all control, shrieked. "I said, get out of my business."

Maggie felt a faint flicker of a smile cross her face; a smile she knew Geraldine saw. "No, I will not — and do you want to know why?"

Geraldine was silent, rooted to her chair, hands grasping the edge of her desk.

"Let me tell you." Maggie walked forward and resting her hands on the desk, she leaned towards the woman who had come so close to ruining everything; so close to returning her to the misery she had escaped. "You see there is a place for me here, Geraldine. And what I didn't know until very recently is that there always has been."

Geraldine leapt to her feet, her chair falling backwards against the wall. For a moment Maggie thought she would fly at her across the desk, but a faint creak from the office door caught their attention. It swung open slowly to reveal Richard Handley and George Parkinson standing in the doorway.

24

Time For Change

MAGGIE HAD NO IDEA how long Richard Handley and George Parkinson had been outside the door; or how much they had heard.

"I hope we haven't caught you at an inconvenient moment, Geraldine," Richard said, the flicker of anger in his eyes and his set jaw indicating he was aware that they had done just that.

Geraldine fought to regain her self-control. She set her chair upright and sat down, smoothing her skirt beneath her, her back straight and her chin lifted. "Richard, George, how lovely to see you, take a seat. Maggie, go on quickly and get drinks for Mr Handley and Mr Parkinson."

Richard remained standing. "That won't be necessary, Maggie, and please do stay. Geraldine, we wanted to talk to you about your new enterprise in London and wondered how much of your time will be taken away from Langley."

The red blotches on Geraldine's face, which had begun to fade, flared up like traitors eager to betray her.

"What enterprise do you mean?" Her voice sounded thin and scratchy.

"Come now, Geraldine, you didn't think you could keep it a secret forever, did you? It's nothing to be embarrassed about. George came across a new shop in the city. The products were so similar to our own; he thought it would be useful to compare prices."

"Yes, it does look impressive, Geraldine. I called in again and saw you there, though you didn't see me," George said. His voice was calm, but Maggie could see irritation in his eyes.

"I wasn't hiding it from anyone. It is simply my own shop and there is no need for anyone to know about it. You can hardly call it competition." Geraldine's tone was defensive.

"Of course, you are right. That is so long as you are handling it in your own time – and, how shall I put it, there is no blurring of lines between the two businesses," Richard said.

"I have no idea what you are referring to but I am beginning to take offence. If you have accusations to make, I suggest you make them. I would also prefer that we didn't have this conversation in front of my staff."

Maggie knew little of Richard Handley. Now as she watched this diminutive man, with worn jacket and deep, cool voice standing before Geraldine, he exuded authority.

"I'm not making accusations, Geraldine; I am merely pointing out the truth. When George saw you, it turned out to be the same day you had an appointment here with my wife. I put two and two together when she told me you had not been able to keep that appointment because your child was ill."

Geraldine rose to her feet. Rage flashed once more in her green eyes, but Maggie could also see a hint of panic. She was not used to feeling trapped.

"Are you questioning whether or not my child was ill? As it happened, I had to take her to see a specialist at a London hospital – not that it is any business of yours, Richard, or anyone else's. I called at the shop on the way back."

"I'm sorry to hear that," Richard said, his voice low.

Now Geraldine's actions, her disappearances for days on end became clear to Maggie. *Don't listen,* she thought, *she's lying – don't fall for it.*

Richard's eyes remained steady, meeting Geraldine's hostile stare. "I hope it isn't serious, but if you need further time off, please let me know beforehand."

There followed a silent stand-off, which to Maggie seemed never-ending. Ash from the cigarette that Geraldine had thrown down on the desk dropped onto the leather, a thin curl of smoke rising from it. The wind battered at the windows again forcing a cold draught through the old frames. At that moment, a breathless Christina reappeared at the office door.

"Oh, there you are, dear, I was looking for you."

"Yes, we seem to have a situation." Richard remained unruffled. "Do you remember how Geraldine missed her appointment to see the furniture supplier with you?"

"Yes, one of her children was ill. Maggie helped me instead."

"So it seems. It also turns out Geraldine was busy sorting out her private business in London; she has a new shop," Richard said, ignoring Geraldine's explanation.

"That's annoying, considering what you said to me a few moments ago – how did you put it, Geraldine – something about my whimsy and lack of experience putting the business at risk?" Christina said, her pale face reddening.

Maggie watched with fascination as Geraldine struggled to decide which tack to take. When Geraldine spoke, she was still on the offensive. She ignored Christina and addressed Richard.

"I've explained what happened and that should be enough. I'm offended you are even raising it."

"I find it offensive that you feel you can speak to my wife in that way. But we will deal with that separately. There is something else I want to talk to you about. Some of the items in your shop are identical to the products you have altered on the last two stocktakes here. Our accountant was concerned and George has investigated it for me."

"So now you are accusing me of stealing?" Geraldine rose to her feet, her voice incredulous. "How dare you." She pointed at Maggie. "I presume you have listened to her lies. I can tell you that I have already sacked her. Now, especially after everything I've done for you, I expect an apology."

She glared at the two men and silence fell over the room once more. No apology came.

Richard walked to the window and looked out as though taking time to consider the next move. He stood, hands behind his back, rocking back and forth on his heels to a slow rhythm. Then he turned to Geraldine.

"Firstly, neither George nor I have spoken to Maggie about you, and she has not come to us. If I have concerns about how the business is being run, I have a right to raise them. Secondly, you are correct. You have done a great deal for us and we have relied on you. I think now we have done so too much. You are a woman of many talents, but it seems to me that honesty and decency are not among them."

Richard walked back from the window towards Christina and standing protectively in front of her, faced Geraldine. "I know how you have spoken to my wife and to George in the past and I have been unwise to ignore it. Just now I witnessed how you speak to Maggie. In case you were wondering, we heard much of what you had to say. You have been proficient in hiding your true nature from me for too long. The only apologies due here are from you – both to Maggie and to my wife."

Richard turned to Maggie, his face serious. "Maggie, you are right – there is a place for you here and I hope that will be the case for many years to come." His gaze fell back on Geraldine. "There is, however, not necessarily a place for everyone."

He turned to leave, with George and Christina following.

Geraldine was reeling as the enormity of her mistake dawned on her, but still she refused to be humbled. Maggie watched as she walked briskly after them, her head held high.

"Richard, Christina," Geraldine called after the group as they stepped out into the corridor, "I'm sure we can work this misunderstanding out."

Richard turned back and spoke before Geraldine could utter another word. "The only misunderstanding, Geraldine, is that you believed this business was your own. It is not. And for the remainder of the short time you have left with us, it's Mr and Mrs Handley to you."

Maggie walked through the great hall. The hail showers had passed over and weak winter sunshine streamed in through the high windows. Geraldine had already left. She had thrown her personal possessions into a bag and stormed out, announcing she would never set foot in the manor again. It seemed to Maggie that with her passing, the old house had let out a long-held breath, and now seemed brighter and airier than before.

Maggie collected Rupert from Keeper's Cottage and walked to the edge of the marsh. She needed fresh air after the drama of the morning. It was hard to believe that Geraldine had gone – that she wouldn't be back. It was harder to believe that she didn't care one way or the other. Any power Geraldine had held over her had vanished like a broken spell.

She sat quietly on a seat by the reed beds. The birds were chattering in readiness for a still distant spring – aware of better times to come. Maggie smiled to herself. On this cold, drab day she realised her new life had truly begun and all she could see was light and colour.

25

The Bittern's Call

MAGGIE STEPPED OUT INTO the morning sunshine. She closed the cottage door behind her and took a deep breath. She had looked forward to and dreaded this day in equal measures. Now she hesitated on the doorstep, placing a hand on the wall; patting it like an old friend. The rough surface had absorbed the spring sunshine and was already warm. The bright light catching the back of her hand revealed prominent blue veins through skin criss-crossed with fine lines. She didn't feel old.

It was a spectacular morning. Spring had come early and the garden shone yellow with daffodils and primulas. The trees and shrubs Maggie and Phil had planted were in blossom, and the lush lawn was already in need of another cut. Contented chickens could be heard clucking and scratching in their enclosure beyond the top of the garden, and every tree and bush seemed alive with chattering birds.

Maggie gazed across the garden and, just for a fleeting moment, she could picture it clearly, as it had been when she'd first laid eyes on it, overgrown and neglected, the leaning yew tree waiting to give up its secret.

So many years had passed since those extraordinary forces of fate had guided her here. How could she ever have imagined the experiences that would follow her arrival – events that had shaped her future?

She sat on the garden seat and stretched out her legs, letting the sun penetrate her flesh and bones as it did the stone walls. She had enough time before her appointment – she could delay it a little while longer. Leaning back, she closed her eyes, allowing the memories to flood in. How easily she could summon pictures of the past; of that frightened woman, so young and yet already scarred and worn down by life. With those images came the stinging memory of fear and loss. She wished she could travel back through time and speak to her; reassure her and give her courage to face the future. But of course the girl had found courage – and it had come from a most unexpected source.

Just then, Maggie caught a peculiar sound on the breeze. After an absence of over a hundred years, the birds had returned to the marshes ten years before. She turned her head in the direction of the reed beds and listened to the bittern's call, remembering the first time she'd heard it – then it had been a call from across time; a call that had heralded the start of a new life for her.

She looked back to the garden and imagined Joseph standing there with his dog at his side by the old yew tree.

Maggie had not seen him for nearly forty years. In that time she'd had many strange dreams. They were so completely different from a normal dream. The detail was incredible, where sight and smell and touch were brought to life with such clarity that she knew they were memories from lives lived before. And during the daytime, when least expected, she would hear a voice or detect a smell that took her to a place somewhere on the far edge of memory. But those recaptured moments had lessened over time. She had wondered if the contentment she had discovered had taken away the gift of seeing through past eyes.

She thought of Joseph again and spoke to him. "Mary had a chance to come back and live here again, Joseph – and she's had such a good life." Her words weren't a calling to a man long dead; they were a statement of fact. She had been privileged to discover something few would ever know or believe. It was a precious secret that she had kept to herself, even from Phil and Anne, and she held it close to her heart.

She looked at her watch. It was time to go. She drove the mile to the manor and entered the familiar old house. She knew she was wanted in the great hall, but instead she diverted towards her office. The antique desk had been repositioned and she had added a few of her own touches over the decades, but it was much as it had been back then. It seemed a lifetime ago since Geraldine had walked out of that room for the last time – it was a lifetime ago.

As she made a final check to ensure all was left neat and tidy, there was a gentle knock at the door. A young woman entered shyly.

"Everyone is ready, Mrs Sheldon."

"Thank you," Maggie said. "I will be down in a moment."

She made her way slowly down the narrow stairs and back along the corridors and past the portraits she had come to know so well. She stood before the double doors into the great hall of Langley Manor, and with her hand on the doorknob she hesitated, looking skyward.

"You were right, Anne," she whispered. "I did have it in me after all."

She pushed the door open to an eruption of spontaneous cheering and applause for the retiring manager of Langley. She gazed through misting eyes across the sea of familiar faces, until she spotted them and her heart filled with pride. *'It wouldn't hurt for you to contact her…'* she'd said after Phil had told her about the mother of his child. He had, and from that small seed of reconciliation, the little boy, Steven, had become part of their lives.

Phil had gone on ahead so that he could be there with their family, to welcome her. There he stood, with his thick grey hair as unruly as ever and his dark eyes shining. At his side were Steven and his wife Emily, and their four children. To Maggie they were her grandchildren and she loved them as if they were her own. If only Anne could have been there, too. It was ten years since her friend had passed away and she still missed her.

When the main celebration was over, with most people returning to their jobs, and Phil and the rest of the family chatting to James Handley – son of Richard and Christina and present owner of Langley, Maggie slipped away to be alone for a minute or two.

Could it really be so long since she had first found Langley? she thought, though, of course, she knew it was Langley that had found her. She had been a lost soul searching for meaning to a life that had no purpose and no joy – and she had found it. More than that, she had found herself.

As she looked out through leaded windows across the river to the bank from where she had first gazed at the manor, strong arms enveloped her from behind. She turned round, mopping the tears from her face.

"I heard the bittern this morning. I love to hear them – they remind me of the first day I came here."

"How about a walk?" Phil said, smiling at his wife and kissing her on the cheek. "I know a lovely place in the wood with a great view – it's a very special place."

Maggie took his hand. "Yes," she said. "It is."